THE SECRET DIARIES

2: Betrayal

Dear Diary,

How is it possible to be happy when I know so much is wrong? Maybe the reason I can be happy is that I didn't know Laurie. Even though I know her body is rotting somewhere, she seems unreal, like somebody I've read about in a magazine. It's only because her death is a threat to Penn that it frightens me.

I keep thinking of Penn handing that money to Casey. Penn was paying him to keep his mouth shut! I saw the way Casey's greedy eyes glittered as each bill came out of Penn's wallet. He's bound to think there's more where that came from. Can't Penn see how dangerous that is? Casey knows all about Laurie's death. How much money will it take to keep him quiet?

Dare you unlock

THE SECRET DIARIES

I
Temptation

II
Betrayal

III
Escape

THE *Point* SECRET DIARIES

2: *Betrayal*

Janice Harrell

■SCHOLASTIC

Scholastic Publications Ltd,
7-9 Pratt Street, London NW1 0AE, UK
a division of Scholastic Publications Limited
London ~ New York ~ Toronto ~ Sydney ~ Auckland

First published in the US by Scholastic Inc., 1994
First published in the UK by Scholastic Publications Ltd, 1995

Copyright © Daniel Weiss Associates, Inc., and Janice Harrell, 1994
Cover illustration copyright © Steiner Lund, 1995
Bullet holes courtesy of Wiltshire Shooting Centre

Produced by Daniel Weiss Associates, Inc.
33 West 17th Street, New York, NY 10011

ISBN 0 590 55948 6

Printed by Cox and Wyman Ltd, Reading, Berks

10 9 8 7 6 5 4 3 2 1

One

Dear Diary,

"I love Penn Parrish." I wrote that weeks ago. It's true now more than ever. But I'm scared, Diary. I wake up at three in the morning with the shakes, my skin clammy. While I was sick with the flu, Penn told me something terrible, and ever since, I've been having the same nightmare over and over. In it a girl is falling, clawing at the air, her mouth open, her eyes wide in terror. She seems to fall for a long time. Then she strikes the rocks of the riverbed with a thud, and her head snaps to an unnatural angle. She lies there, face to the sky, and the shallow water moves her wispy hair.

1

*The worst part is waking up. Then I
realize that the nightmare is real. Laurie
Jenkins is dead.*

For years I've written my diary in code. It's a
hangover from the sixth grade, when I thought my
parents were spying on me. Stupid. But now I'm
glad my diary is secret. If it weren't, I could never
write the truth. It would be far too dangerous.

Saturday morning my father was snoring in
his room at the back of the house. He had come
back sunburned from a Caribbean vacation,
bringing with him painted coconuts and a floppy
hat made of woven palm fronds. I might have
felt jealous of his vacation if I hadn't been so excited about spending the weekend at Penn's
cabin out in the woods. The entire gang would
be there, and it was good to be included. But
what made my heart beat hard, and made me
press my cold hand against my suddenly flushed
cheeks, was the thought that I would be with
Penn.

Noticing my hand was trembling, I put down
my cup of cocoa. On the pond outside, a mallard
reared, quacking angrily, and then settled back
on the water in a flutter of ruffled feathers. I
could see the few golf carts that were already out

on the golf course. Small in the distance, they darted, beetlelike, by the orange flag fluttering over the green.

A few muffin crumbs floated on the surface of the greasy water in the kitchen sink. I turned away, feeling weak in the knees. It's because I've just gotten over the flu, I told myself. That's all.

I opened the living-room window, and suddenly I heard the roar of Penn's Corvette. It seemed to take a long time to get my overnight bag. It was odd that my heart was racing, but my legs refused to respond. I pushed the door open and grasped the handle of the bag. "I'm all right," I said aloud. "I'm only tired."

I saw the red convertible pulling into the driveway. Stumbling down the steps, I let my overnight bag fall from my grasp as I watched the car door open. Sunshine picked out platinum strands in Penn's ash-blond hair and gave it fire. Beautiful! I thought, catching my breath suddenly. I wanted to cradle his head in my hands and kiss him. I imagined us walking on the beach, picking wildflowers and drinking champagne like lovers in a corny movie. I suppose I must have been woozy, because for a fraction of a second that plan seemed practical. He put his hands on either side of my waist. "Are you okay?" he asked. "You're so pale."

I grinned foolishly—the sight of him had that effect on me. "Just the postviral blahs."

"You'd better take it easy. How was your father's vacation?" It was Penn who had nursed me through the flu, while my father was having fun in the islands. Dad had an uncanny knack for disappearing whenever I needed him.

"He did some snorkeling," I said, "got sunburn, and drank margaritas. That was about all he told me." Penn opened the door for me, and I fell against the soft leather of the bucket seat. "I wonder if I'll ever see this Jennifer person he goes out with," I said.

The car backed slowly out of the driveway. Then Penn pressed his foot down firmly on the accelerator, as if he had been granted lifetime immunity from speed limits. "Maybe she doesn't even exist," he said. "Maybe all the time your dad says he's with her, he's really curled up with a set of blueprints."

"Maybe he's lying to her about his age," I said. "He might not want to let on that he's old enough to have a seventeen-year-old daughter. I'll bet that's why he's not bringing her around."

At the side of the main road, a man in a business suit stood next to a German shepherd that was lying on the ground. My hand went to my mouth. There was a loud buzzing in my ears. The dog was breathing, but his middle was flat.

"Don't look," said Penn, speeding past.

I gasped for breath. I could still see the dog, even though my eyes were now closed.

"Are you all right?" Penn's hand rested on my knee.

I felt dizzy. "Yes, I'll be okay in a minute," I insisted.

I let my head drop back against the seat. The music from the car radio began to blend with the hum of the car's engine and with Penn's voice. . . . A videotape had begun in my head that I was powerless to stop. In it, a girl is falling, clawing at the air, her mouth open, her eyes wide in terror. It was the familiar nightmare.

"Knock-knock-knocking on heaven's door," sang a monotonous whine on the radio. I jerked suddenly, startled by the sound.

"You were falling asleep," Penn said. He tossed me his jacket. "Here, use this for a pillow."

I shook my head. "No. I'm awake." I was afraid of what I might dream if I fell asleep. But even with my eyes wide open and focused on the road ahead of us, the images and noises in my

head would not stop. . . . There is a crackling
sound as the girl's body, soft at the surface like
Jell-O, is rolled by rubber-gloved hands onto a
black plastic tarp. The long black bundle is lifted
and awkwardly jackknifed until it will fit in a car
trunk. The trunk slams shut with a whoosh of air
and the solid sound of metal meeting metal.

The car, its lights turned low, bumps precariously along a deserted logging road, striking
stones and fallen tree limbs as it goes. At last it
stops and dark figures pull the bundled tarp out
of the trunk. They breathe heavily with fear and
with the effort needed for their grisly task. "Be
careful," cries a familiar voice. Dry branches
break and the dead leaves of the forest crack and
crumble under their feet. They lower their grisly
burden to the ground, then roll the softening
body out onto the leaves. They frantically bunch
the black plastic tarp up. With their bare hands
looking like flashes of white in the light reflected
from the night sky, they scoop up handfuls of
leaves and throw them on top of the body. "Let's
get out of here," says a panicked whisper. Tossed
leaves fall gently and an open white hand lying
on the ground, the last trace of the body, disappears. "I feel sick," says a voice.

"You can't be sick now," someone responds.

The little car's motor coughs as it goes back the way it came, bumping over obstacles in the abandoned road.

Funny thing. The next image is less vivid, though this was the scene I actually saw. The flames devouring a car are yellow and ravenous. It burns like a meteor. The fireball is destroying all traces of evidence of the body. Now no one will ever know. No one but four loyal friends. And me, Joanna Rigsby.

I turned off Penn's radio with a sharp snap of my wrist. "Do you think things you just hear about can be more real than things you actually experience?"

Penn's eyebrows lifted. "Is this a loaded question?"

"Not really." I shrugged.

Penn must have known I was thinking of Laurie Jenkins's death, but he didn't let on. It was better if we didn't talk about it. I knew that. I only wished I could quit thinking about it and could get rid of my nightmares. Ahead, a gap in the trees marked the turnoff to the cabin. When Penn turned into the dirt driveway, I saw that we were the last of the group to arrive. Two cars were out front, and our friends were sitting on the steps waiting for us. On the top step was

Casey MacNamara. He was pale, as was fitting to a computer geek. With his white face and thatch of carroty hair, he was a regular fixture at the school's computer lab, which he ran like his private kingdom. On the bottom step, side by side sat Tessa West and Stephen Garner, looking amazingly alike. I wondered sometimes if that was why they felt such a strong attraction to each other. Wasn't there a Greek myth about a guy who fell in love with his own reflection? That story could have been about Stephen and Tessa. Their baggy clothes gave them each a sagging, street-person look, but a close glance showed that they were startlingly attractive in precisely the same way—untidy dark hair, damp, brilliant eyes, and carefully modeled chins and noses.

Penn got out of the car. "I thought I told you we were going to be late," he said apologetically. "Joanna is still trying to shake off the flu."

"I needed to sleep in," I added.

"You could have given us a key," Casey snapped. "We could have gone in and lit a fire instead of freezing our butts off out here."

Penn ignored Casey's remark and began unloading the trunk. He loved this house in the woods; his parents had built it by hand back in

the days when they were happily married. The
place was full of good memories. No way was
Penn going to give Casey a key.

Penn unlocked the door and pushed it
open. Stepping inside, I felt a rush of happi-
ness that almost took my breath away. Light
spilled in the windows; the living room was almost entirely enclosed by glass. A pool of yellow sunshine warmed the wood floor in front
of the window. The floor was bleached a
lighter shade where the light fell. Slanting
shafts of sun picked out floating specks of
dust, and set ablaze the copper bottoms of the
pans hung in the kitchen. A river ran behind
the house, and beyond that, tall green pines
and maples showed the first reddish bud of
leaves.

Well-thumbed books filled the small bookcase
beside the fireplace. Fat roses decorated the
chintz on the sofa and chairs, and a pack of cards
lay facedown on the low table in front of the
couch.

I hoped this weekend was going to be easier
than the last one. Then, Casey had brought a
portable record player and had insisted on playing an annoying French song over and over. It
grated on everyone's nerves, and Penn had had

to restrain Stephen from attacking Casey at one point.

I let my bag fall against the back of the sofa, and dropped onto the soft cushions, my nose pressed against a chintz rose. I could hear chatter and the opening and closing of the front door as the others carried things in from their cars. Tessa laid a physics book on the low table beside me. I involuntarily winced. If it hadn't been for Stephen and Tessa's efforts, I would have been flunking physics. As it was, I was barely scraping by, and missing three days with the flu was not going to help.

"My record!" screeched Casey. "How'd it end up over there?" I propped myself up awkwardly on my elbows. A record cover rested against the big northern window. On it was a picture of a French cabaret singer sketched in purple and black. It was the record Casey had played endlessly. "Damn," said Casey, snatching it up. "With the sun coming in on it like that, it could have gotten warped."

Tessa's and Stephen's eyes met briefly, and I knew suddenly that it was no accident the record had been left leaning against the sunny window. "It'll be all right," said Stephen coolly. "It's not like you left it in the car or anything."

Casey slid the record out of its jacket and put it on the record player. "It looks wavy!" he mourned. "I'll bet it's ruined."

The singer's voice rang out in a wavering parody of itself.

Casey snatched the needle off the record with an angry scratching sound. "Who put my record by the window?" he demanded. "It wasn't me."

Penn shrugged. "You remember how we were all rushing around when we left last time. Anybody could have stuck it there to get it out of the way."

"You guys did it on purpose," yelled Casey. "You were all complaining about the record. I guess you decided to do something about it, didn't you? Didn't you?"

"Don't be paranoid, Casey," said Tessa. "If we wanted to get rid of your record, it would have been easier just to step on it."

If I hadn't seen that quick glance between Tessa and Stephen, I might have thought she was telling the truth.

"Tell you what," said Penn. "I'll pay you for the record. Fair enough?"

"That record is valuable," Casey muttered. "It's a collector's item. It'll probably cost me fifty bucks to get another one."

We all knew he had found the old record in
his family's garage. Penn, his face wooden,
peeled two twenties and a ten off a stack of bills
and laid them on Casey's open palm. Then he
took the record off the phonograph, dropped it
on the floor, and stepped on it. I heard the plastic crack.

"Hey, why'd you do that?" Casey cried.

"You said yourself it was ruined," said Penn.

"Yeah, but it had sentimental value!"

"You've got the record jacket to remember it
by," said Penn, turning away.

After that, the weekend fell into its familiar
pattern. Tessa, as usual, got projects going. There
were fires to build, games to play, fancy food to
prepare. Tessa never liked to sit still for long.
Stephen had brought a gun he'd found in a trunk
in his family's attic, and for a while we tried target practice against an old outhouse. Stephen
drew three concentric circles on its door with a
Magic Marker and made cross-hatched lines on
the smallest circle to indicate the bull's-eye. I
hated the noise of the gun, and when my turn
came, I squeezed my eyes shut as I pulled the
trigger. The pistol leapt in my hands, and there
was an explosion that made my ears ring
painfully.

"Stop her," cried Casey. "She's a menace."

When I opened my eyes, I was embarrassed to see that my bullet had missed the outhouse altogether and put a round black hole in a pine tree five feet to its left. Blushing hotly, I handed the gun to Stephen. I watched, humbled, as he hit one bull's-eye after another.

We took walks in the woods. The first hint of unfolding leaves had appeared overhead on the bare branches, and sun glittered on the river, throwing odd moving patterns against the tree trunks. The moss smelled damp. I fell behind the others, too tired to keep pace, and Penn stayed with me. We sat on a damp fallen tree trunk, and after a few minutes I felt the wet sinking into the seat of my jeans. He touched the corner of my mouth with his finger and smiled. Overcome with peace and contentment, I let my head fall against the hollow of his shoulder.

"I wish we could stay here forever," I said. He stroked my hair, and I listened to my breath whistling gently against his shirt. "I wish the rest of the world didn't even exist," I added.

"I wish a lot of things," he said.

Laurie. Neither of us could seem to stop thinking about Laurie.

Once I was rested, we walked back to the cabin. It was quiet without the others, and when we stepped over the threshold, I felt as if the house were asleep. It was so peaceful in the cabin, with the golden light spilling in the window.

I stretched out on the couch at once, thankful not to be walking.

Penn smiled and squeezed onto the couch next to me. There wasn't enough room for both of us to lie on it, and he had his hand on the floor for balance to keep from falling off. "Ditch the back cushions," he said, "so we'll have more room." He bumped his head on the coffee table. "Ouch." He rubbed it.

"This isn't going to work," I said, laughing.

"Sure it will, it's nice and cozy." Penn grabbed at the table with one hand for balance, and managed to land a kiss on my lips.

"You're going to fall off!" I protested.

We heard voices, and suddenly Penn fell off the couch. I sat bolt upright, and he hastily got up and sat down beside me.

Casey threw the door open.

"My, my, my," he said. "Looks as if you two could stand to comb your hair. What could you guys have been doing on the couch that would get your hair so messed up? Studying physics?"

"Anybody for lunch?" asked Tessa quickly. "Penn, why don't you wash the lettuce. Casey, I've got a treat for you."

"Chocolate mousse?" He perked up hopefully.

Casey's mean streak always caught me off balance, and it was surprisingly hard for me to laugh off his teasing.

Later I fell asleep over my physics book, but I was pleasantly conscious of the bustle of activity around me. I can see Tessa now, if I close my eyes, leaping up from our quiet circle around the fire: "Let's play poker—deuces, one-eyed jacks, suicide kings, and the man with the ax are wild," she would call cheerfully. She loved to cook and was continually getting us to help with the food. We picked the meat out of walnuts, shelled peas, shucked corn.

I spent a lot of time writing in my diary. Once or twice I had caught the others staring at the open pages, trying to make sense of the jumbled letters. I think they looked on my diary as one of my eccentricities, like my habit of scraping whipped cream off of hot chocolate and picking the nuts out of brownies.

"I am happy," I wrote that weekend. As I

stared at the jumbled letters on the page, they easily rearranged themselves in my mind into English.

> ... How is it possible to be happy when I know so much is wrong? Maybe the reason I can be happy is that I didn't know Laurie. Even though I know her body is rotting somewhere, she seems unreal, like somebody I've read about in a magazine. It's only because her death is a threat to the people I care about that it frightens me.
>
> I keep thinking of Penn handing those bills to Casey. Penn was paying him for that awful record! I saw the way Casey's greedy eyes glittered as each bill came out of Penn's wallet. He's bound to think there's more where that came from. Can't Penn see how dangerous that is? Casey knows all about Laurie's death. What if he wants money for keeping his mouth shut about that? Next time, fifty dollars isn't going to be enough.

Two

Dear Diary,

It seems odd that the others are going on as if nothing has happened. It's hard for me to write this, even in my private code, because it suggests that my friends are heartless, and I know that isn't true. They've been so nice to me—the hot chicken soup Tessa brought me, Penn tenderly sponging my forehead and wiping my mouth when I was sick, Stephen's endless patience coaching me in physics.

I know they'd have grieved for Laurie if they hadn't been desperate to save themselves. But however much they liked Laurie—and let's be honest, perhaps just before she died, she had got on their

*nerves—they have no intention of facing a
public trial and risking being sent to prison
for twenty years for her sake. So Penn
faked a letter from Laurie to her mom. He
forged Laurie's signature, then drove five
hours, to Washington, D.C., and mailed it
from there. So, officially, Laurie's still alive.
The police search was called off, and
everyone thinks she's run away and is
working at some low-paying job in the city.
If her friends act upset, it would look suspicious. They have to behave as if they think
Laurie is okay. . . .*

If her friends made a kind of uneasy peace
with Laurie's death, Bobby Jenkins had not. He
was Laurie's stepbrother, but what went on between them was more than simple family feeling. Once, when I was at a party at his house, I
had found a book in his bookcase. It was in-
scribed, "To Bobby, with all my heart and soul
forever. Laurie." Bobby lived across the street
from me and sometimes I saw him out washing
his car. He was a big guy, but not all muscles.
More like a football player who's gotten out of
shape. He generally went around in grungy old
T-shirts and seldom-washed jeans, with his un-

combed hair pulled into a tiny ponytail, but he was fussy about his car. I often saw him scrubbing at it, scowling into its shiny surface as if dismayed by his own fierce reflection.

Now that I knew what had happened to Laurie, I was nervous and guilty around him. I despised myself when I heard the forced tone that had somehow crept into my casual hellos. Once I had watched Bobby lift a large boy over his head and pitch him over a high railing at school, so I had some reason to be nervous. I knew Bobby could be violent.

I smiled vaguely at him when I went out to the street to pick up the mail.

"Hey!" he grunted. This was Bobby's customary greeting, and I froze, my smile growing stiff on my lips.

He came across the street toward me, Laurie's Irish setter bounding after him. "Down, Blue," he commanded. A wet T-shirt clung to the round contours of his vast chest. "You got Baker for history?" he asked.

I nodded.

"I'm going to be away for a while." He scratched his head. "Maybe I can get your notes from class when I get back."

I was amazed that Bobby worried about taking notes in class. I had never seen him show any interest in school. In fact, it was hard to imagine him with a book or a book bag or using a writing instrument of any kind. "Sure." I gulped. "Where're you going?"

"I'm going to D.C. His face darkened. "I'm going to look for Laurie."

"But you'll never find her!" I burst out. Then, aware of how odd that sounded, at least to my own guilty ears, I added hastily, "Washington is a big city. She could be anywhere."

"Down, Blue," he said angrily. The setter retreated to a safe distance and began sniffing at a tuft of grass. "I'm sure not going to find her sitting around here, so I better give it a try. I'm going to start by going to divey bars and dumpy little food places. That's got to be the kind of place she's working."

When he rolled his eyes to look at Blue, I saw that the whites of his eyes were bloodshot.

"I don't think that's such a good idea," I said faintly.

"You think I'm better off sitting around here staring at the four walls?" he challenged me. "Well, I'm not! I'm going to have it out with her. Let her tell me to my face that she doesn't want to see me anymore, if that's the way she feels."

His eyes filled up with tears. He turned suddenly on his heels with an impatient gesture. "Come on, Blue."

I watched as he stomped away and up his front steps, shooed the dog in the door, and slammed the door shut behind him.

I was so distressed at the notion of Bobby wandering hopelessly from one dingy restaurant to another that I only dimly became aware of the roaring in my ears.

I jerked around suddenly to face a noise that sounded like the earth being torn in half. Two people on a huge motorcycle were heading directly for me. The bike's motor sputtered, and the cyclist put out his leg to keep it from falling over. He pulled off his black helmet to reveal Stephen's radiant face. Tessa took off her helmet and slid off the back of the bike. "You wouldn't believe how terrifying it is riding on that thing," she gasped. "My whole life flashed before my eyes, I promise you."

"I got a really good deal on it," said Stephen. "When the owner's wife had a baby, she made him sell it."

"Smart woman," said Tessa.

I knew that Stephen had been without wheels since his car had burned one night at the gas station. I had been told that the insurance money had been disappointing. The bike presumably was the answer to his transportation problem.

"I love it," he said. "It's a completely new experience—the vibration, the noise."

"The terror," put in Tessa.

"She isn't used to it yet," said Stephen.

"Of course, we've still got my car for serious trips," Tessa said. "The bike is more like a toy."

"Tessa's going to learn to like it as much as I do," Stephen said. "Hop on, Joanna. I'll give you a ride. Keep your leg off the exhaust pipe and hold on tight, that's all there is to it."

I backed off. "That's okay. I'll take your word for it. I'm still feeling kind of wobbly. I just got over the flu."

He didn't argue with me. It is very possible that I looked as sick as I felt, especially after my chat with Bobby.

"We're on our way to The Bakery," said Stephen. "Want to come? We ran into Penn and Casey at the library, and we told them we'd get you."

"Sure."

"I'm riding with Joanna," Tessa said.

"You're missing out," Stephen wheedled.

"We'll see you there, macho man," said Tessa.

"Low blow!" Stephen protested. "And it's not a macho thing. Bikes are ecologically amazing. You want to guess how many miles this baby gets to the gallon?"

"Let me get my keys," I said.

Moments later we were in my car, moving at a sedate pace toward The Bakery. We could hear Stephen's motorcycle roaring behind us. Boys' taste in transportation amazes me. "It gets me there and takes me back" was my idea of a good sort of car. But Stephen and Penn went for lots of noise and horsepower. I had the idea that for them, getting there came second.

"Bobby's going to D.C. to look for Laurie," I said.

Tessa darted a quick glance at me. "You didn't tell him anything, did you?"

"How could I? I did point out that he was never going to find her."

"Well, that's true enough." Tessa sighed.

I remembered that Tessa had helped carry Laurie's rotting body into the woods, wrapped in a tarp. With her own hands, the same well-shaped, pale hands I was now gazing at, she had covered Laurie's dead body with leaves. How could she sit there so coolly saying that Bobby wouldn't find Laurie in Washington, as if he simply had the wrong address? I shivered and looked away. "He's going to go to one little greasy spoon after another in the hope he'll find her washing dishes or waiting tables at one of them," I said.

"How long does he plan to do this?" Tessa asked. "A year? Two? There are a lot of places to wait tables in Washington, D.C."

"Bobby doesn't think—he acts. I expect he'll come back in a few days. I just hope he doesn't end up getting mugged first," I said.

"It'd have to be a brave mugger to go after Bobby," said Tessa.

"Why didn't Penn come by to get me himself?" I asked.

Tessa grimaced. "He's on Casey detail. We've decided we need to make a special effort to pay attention to Casey to make him feel important. It's the only thing we can think of—lots of tender loving care. Penn is patient, but unfortunately he doesn't know how to flatter. That's where I come in. Casey eats up flattery."

. . . It was Casey's fault to begin with! That's what makes me mad. It was his idea

to erase the C Stephen got in history and replace it with an A. He knew Stephen was terrified the C would keep him out of Princeton. So Casey offered to "help him out." It was easy for him, since he had actually written most of the school's computer programs. A touch of the key, and zip! Suddenly Stephen had an A instead of a C in ninth-grade English.

Casey loves to show off what he can do on the computer. Worse, he finds out where somebody's weak spot is and then he zeroes in on it. Unfortunately, Penn's weak spot is obvious. He has a problem obeying speed limits. He was on the verge of losing his license until Casey tinkered with the Department of Transportation's records. Then, poof! Penn's tickets vanished. Suddenly his record was clean. I know Penn was wrong to let Casey do that for him, but the point is, it was all Casey's idea in the first place. Not that he would admit it. Casey remembers only what he wants to remember. I've even heard him preach on the importance of law and order!

Maybe it would have blown over, but Casey had to brag about it to Laurie.

*Showing off again. When Laurie screamed
she was going to turn them all in, I guess
Stephen sort of lost it. Penn said there was a
lot of shouting and shoving, and the next
thing anyone knew, Laurie had tumbled off
the cliff.*

*   Horrible! To go out for a picnic on a
sunny day and suddenly to die! But it was
an accident. I have to keep reminding myself
of that. None of them meant for Laurie to
die. . . .*

Tessa and I arrived at The Bakery to find
Penn and Casey waiting for us at a table by a
window. The slanting afternoon sun highlighted
the texture of the brick wall. Around the room
were posters advertising folk festivals and music
workshops, interspersed with charcoal sketches
and signs about the environment. Sprigs of flow-
ering chive in small bottles stood on the tables.
The Bakery was owned by a potbellied, pony-
tailed man named George who had been an old
college friend of Penn's mother. It specialized in
fresh breads, gourmet salads, herb teas, and a
varied assortment of sinfully fattening cookies
and pastries.

"If it isn't Tessa and Joanna the Silent," said

Casey. "Where's Stephen, Tessa? I thought you two were joined at the hip."

Tessa pulled out a chair and sat down. "He's outside attending to the care and feeding of his new bike."

Stephen burst in just then, peeling off his black-leather jacket and gloves. "The bike was coughing on the way over," he said. "I wonder if it's a spark plug or the fuel system."

"Don't ask me," said Casey. "I don't know anything about small engines. But maybe Joanna did bike repairs in her former life." His voice sank to a whisper. "What about it, Joanna? Is that one of your dark secrets?"

I ignored him. Stephen went up to the counter and came back with steaming cups of peppermint tea and a basket heaped with hard rolls.

Casey leaned back in his chair. "I think I could eat a Linzer tart," he said. "Yep, that'd just about hit the spot."

"Well, why don't you get up and get it?" I asked.

Penn leapt up. "I'll get it. Anybody else want anything?"

Casey squinted. "Hot chocolate, too, Penn, old chum. Have 'em put whipped cream on it and maybe some grated chocolate on top."

A spot of color rose over Penn's cheekbones, but he went to fetch Casey's order. When he came back with it, Casey made no move to pay him.

"You ought to pick up your own check now and then, Casey," I said, "or people are going to think you're a kept man."

I felt a sharp kick under the table and looked at Tessa in surprise.

"Very funny, Joanna," sputtered Casey. "And exactly what is that supposed to mean?" His voice was shrill. "If you weren't a girl, I'd sock you right in the beezus."

Glancing around the table at the frozen faces of my friends, I knew I had made a mistake. "I was only teasing," I said. "I didn't mean anything."

"Can I have a bite of that cookie?" Tessa chimed in nervously. "Casey, where did you get that shirt? I love it."

Casey looked at the shadow stripes of lavender and green on his shirtfront with satisfaction. Considering that he did not rank exactly high in the good-looks department, he was surprisingly vain. "Like it? I got it at Hoffman's. Quality tells, huh?"

"Hundred-percent cotton?" inquired Stephen.

"A blend," Casey admitted. "But I'm thinking of going to a hundred percent if I can get the ironing lined up. You don't want to send a fine piece of clothing to the laundry, you know. I don't know what they do to them there—put them in hot kettles with a few corpses, I guess." He snickered.

The others paled. Casey's little jokes about corpses were not much to anybody's taste, which was hardly surprising under the circumstances.

Eventually the conversation turned to physics, as it had a way of doing. We all had Mr. Dockerty for physics.

Penn scratched a formula on a napkin. "It's a law," he said.

"But why?" asked Casey. "I don't get it."

"It's a law. Just accept it."

"That's not going to be on the test," said Tessa. "He said nothing about quantum mechanics being on the test. He said this stuff was for fun."

"Dockerty has a pretty perverted idea about fun, if you ask me," snorted Casey. "I personally would rather get drunk and carouse with naked ladies." He leaned back precariously in his chair. "Only pretty ones, though. What's the good of an ugly woman?"

"Marie Curie, Rosa Parks, Joan of Arc," I murmured.

Stephen shot me a pleading look. He was obviously afraid I was going to offend Casey. But Casey's self-assurance was unshakable.

"Anything they did a man could have done better if he'd put his mind to it," insisted Casey. "I don't have anything against the weaker sex," he went on, "but we were all better off when they were strictly ornamental." His beady eyes fixed on me. "Say, Joanna, is your mom a career woman?"

I hesitated, suddenly unsure of myself. My fear was that Casey would somehow manage to track down my crazy mother. I hadn't even told Penn about my mother's delusions, and I wasn't about to tell Casey. I had no intention of giving him that kind of ammunition to use against me. I had already seen him torture the others with his continuous harping on the themes of corpses, cliffs, murder.

"My mother has a job," I conceded finally. "I don't know if you'd say she has a career."

"Why do you always have to wait five min-

utes before you answer a simple question?" Casey
asked, his eyes narrowing.

"Some people are thoughtful by nature,
Casey," said Tessa. "Joanna only wished to give
your question her full consideration, I'm sure."

"So what does she do at this job?" Casey
asked, refusing to be sidetracked.

I figured it would be safe enough to tell him.
It's not as if there was a central directory of people who refinish furniture in dingy sweatshops.
There was no way Casey could track down my
mother. "She restores furniture," I said, relaxing
a little.

"She restores furniture, huh? In Raleigh?
That's where you used to live, isn't it?"

I nodded, unable to trust myself to speak. I
had lived in Raleigh once, but it had been when
I was small.

"So, who does she work for?" he asked.

I shrugged.

"You don't remember the name of your mother's employer?" Casey said incredulously. "Isn't
that kind of peculiar? What was it? Krzymisky
Unlimited, or something? All kinds of nonsense
letters like you write in that weird diary of
yours?"

"It's a small operation. I'm not even sure it

has a name. They do contract work for decorators."

Penn leapt up suddenly, and his chair scraped across the rough floor with a protesting howl. "I don't know about the rest of you, but I've got a lot of homework."

I got up, too. Stephen said, "I'll give you a ride, Casey. Wait'll you try my bike. It's an incredible experience. Ask Tessa."

"Enjoy, Casey. I'm riding home with Joanna," said Tessa. "See you, guys."

We fled. Outside, Penn took a step toward me, then hesitated. I knew he felt bad that he had been unable to protect me from Casey's prying questions.

"It's okay," I said.

He gave me a rueful look. "I'll call you."

"Jeez." Tessa got in my car and slammed her door shut. "We made this solemn agreement none of us were going to rock the boat and say anything to tick Casey off, but for a minute there I thought Penn was going to lose it and choke him. He hates it when Casey goes after you."

"I don't think it's anything personal," I said. "Casey goes after everybody."

"It's good you can see that," said Tessa. "I

honestly don't think Casey has any idea how much he gets to people. It's like he's tone deaf when it comes to relationships, you know? It's sort of a disability."

   . . . I disagreed. Casey had a kind of radar that picked up people's tender spots, and when he saw that somebody was squirming, he needled them even harder. I didn't bother to point that out to Tessa. What good would it do? When it came to Casey, we were powerless.

Three

Dear Diary,

Keeping watch on Casey is torture. Listening to him drone on about computers, I find myself daydreaming about rainy days in the Corvette—me and Penn alone. The last thing I want is to be a permanent chaperon, but I don't have any choice. It's the new plan. Penn and I are taking our turn keeping Casey amused. It wouldn't be quite so awful except that Casey doesn't know good food from bad and makes us go to tacky restaurants with fountains of colored water and maitre d's in white jackets. Penn is paying a fortune for us to eat TV dinners reheated in restaurant microwaves.

*   *   *

Sunday, Penn and I sat down to brunch at The Bakery with Casey. At least the food is reliable here, I told myself, recalling the ghastly, pretentious places Casey had dragged us to in the past week.

The Bakery was packed, with a line of waiting patrons that snaked out into the parking lot. Frantic, unkempt waiters, their ponytails stringy and half undone, went up and down the line taking orders in a futile effort to try to speed the flow. We had snagged a desirable table in a corner, slightly away from the main crush. The section where we were sitting was elevated a step or two over the rest of the café with a good view of the pleasant Sunday confusion—families, babies slung over parents' shoulders in canvas tot carriers, singles in jeans and horn-rimmed glasses, the entire panorama of the nonchurchgoing population of our town.

Windows ran along two sides of that corner of the restaurant, so the tables were flooded with light, and the smell of coffee and fresh bread filled the air. Casey had ordered blueberry pancakes and, while waiting for them to arrive, had maneuvered Penn into buying him the Sunday paper. He tore through the comics, his

cup of coffee giving off neat curls of steam at
his elbow. "That *Calvin and Hobbes* is a stitch,"
he commented, letting that section drop to the
floor. Then he folded the main section in half
and scanned the front page with desultory interest. Suddenly his eyes widened. "Hey, look
here, you guys. They've found a body in the
woods."

Penn reached for the paper, but Casey tilted
his chair back, leaning out of his reach, and
smiled fiendishly. "Partially decomposed body of
a female," he read aloud. To me his voice
seemed excruciatingly loud, as if he were shouting into a microphone. "Found by a hunter." He
looked up at Penn. "That's funny. I didn't know
anything was in season about now. What could
he have been hunting? Oh, wait a minute. It
says right here. Turkeys. The guy was a turkey
hunter. Seems his dog started digging in the
leaves and the next thing you know, this hunter
is looking at a dead body, or what was left of it.
Bet that made him lose his breakfast, wouldn't
you think?"

A wave of nausea swept over me. When my
frightened gaze found Penn's face, I saw that he
had gone white.

The waiter slid a plate of steaming pancakes

in front of Casey and picked up the wire stand holding the number 3 that marked our table. "Number three—blueberry pancakes?" he asked.

"Right here," said Casey. "Hey, man, I asked for extra syrup."

"You did?" The waiter, a pimply young man wearing small hoop earrings, looked momentarily confused. "Wait a minute. I'll get it."

"I like this place," said Casey as the waiter walked away, "but the waiters stink. Looks like they could wash their necks now and then, too. And those earrings—they make me sick."

Penn was eyeing the newspaper, but he did not make another attempt to grab it. Since I was directly to Casey's right, I could see the headline of the article: BODY OF WOMAN FOUND. Maybe it wasn't Laurie, I thought. After all, women were murdered all the time. My mouth was dry and I forced myself to sip ice water from my sweating glass.

Casey dug his fork into the stack of pancakes and shoveled a bite into his mouth. "Says here that foul play is suspected." He grinned at Penn. "What do you think of that? Foul play. And right here in our fair city. Kind of makes you stop and think. I guess they'll be able to identify the body, all right, even if it's pretty far gone and foxes have been chewing on it, bugs in the guts, the whole nine yards."

We both watched in repelled fascination as Casey shoveled dripping mouthfuls of pancakes into his face. I licked my dry lips.

Penn, seeing that Casey was absorbed in eating his pancakes, quietly reached out his hand for the paper. "Not so fast," said Casey, talking with his mouth full. "I'm not finished with it yet." He put it on the floor beside his chair.

The waiter placed a metal pitcher of syrup beside Casey's plate.

"Wouldn't you think they could identify the body from dental records?" Casey asked.

Penn's eyes involuntarily went to the waiter, but the man's face was impassive. Presumably he heard people discussing the identification of bodies over breakfast every day.

"That would depend," I said. "I don't see how a person could be identified that way if they had perfect teeth. I mean, isn't it done mostly with notes dentists make about where they've put in fillings and crowns? These days lots of kids don't have any fillings at all. I don't, for example."

Casey's eyes widened. "What makes you think the dead person was young? Did I say that?"

I felt my face grow warm. "I was just giving that as an example. Of course, I don't have any idea how they actually identify bodies."

"Naturally," said Casey smoothly. "I may tease you a little bit, but I never figured that you were a mass murderer in your former life, Joanna. But people do have the most amazing secrets. You'd be surprised." He looked at Penn, and the corners of his lips curled up. I suppose he intended to be smiling.

Penn was pale. "I'd like to see that story, Casey."

"Oh, would you? Well, sure. Go ahead. You paid for the paper, didn't you? Seems like they found the body up about three miles north of Lookout Point. Funny, isn't it? I bet you've been up to Lookout Point a hundred times. If you'd gone up the road a bit, you might have driven right past that very body."

He handed the paper to Penn, who read it in silence. I would have loved to lean over his shoulder and read it at the same time, but I knew I had to avoid seeming interested. Casey didn't realize that Penn had told me about Laurie's death, and I intended to keep it that way. He was insufferable enough when he was just "hinting" at what had happened. I hated to think what it would be like if he gave his tongue free rein.

I pushed the food around on my plate and stared out the dusty window that looked onto the porch of the café. A few hardy souls were breakfasting outside in the thin sunshine. A young father bounced a toddler on his knee. An elderly professorial type with a beard was working the *New York Times* crossword puzzle with a ballpoint pen.

"Good grief, you guys are letting your food get cold!" Casey cried.

I met his gaze. "I don't know about you, but talk about decomposing bodies kills my appetite. I'm surprised you can read that stuff and keep feeding your face, Casey."

"What? Aw, nah. It's not like we *knew* her or anything, is it? I mean, heck, everyone has to die sometime. It's as natural as sex and spring-time, you know? Think about it. What could be more natural than a body decaying? It's return-ing to the great compost heap of the earth, you might say."

I felt sick. It must be Laurie's body! I didn't dare let Casey know what I was thinking. I let my hands fall to my lap so that he wouldn't no-tice they were shaking.

Penn scanned the rest of the paper. "I see they're saying Compuwork's new program has a serious bug in it that might damage computers," he said.

Casey blanched. "Hey, gimme that." He snatched the business section back from Penn and began reading it, mumbling phrases aloud. "Unsubstantiated. Probably substandard machines. It's only the condensation feature, anyhow." He heaved a sigh. "Jeez, Penn, don't give me a shock like that when I'm eating."

Penn's eyes met mine in amusement.

Casey had, luckily, brought his own car, so at least after we left the restaurant we were rid of him. Penn's Corvette turned north. "Let's take a drive," he said. "I have to think."

"Do you think it was Laurie's body they found?" I asked.

Penn hesitated. "It's got to be. It's not as if the woods up there are full of bodies."

"Do you think the police can identify her?"

"Probably," he said. "Think of those things you've read about how the army just has a finger bone and six weeks later they've got the guy's name, rank, and serial number. I don't know." He hesitated. "There are ways I could find out more about it. My dad's buddies with this pathologist named Ed Boddie."

I glanced at him quickly.

Penn smiled. "Boddie. It's weird, isn't it? There's a surgeon around here named Payne, too. I wouldn't want to try him. The point is, I could find out a lot more than I know, but I'm afraid it would be a mistake to ask."

"Oh, no! Don't ask!" I cried.

"Don't worry. I'm not going to do anything so stupid. I'm so paranoid, I'm already wondering if there's any way the car could be bugged."

"I don't see how Casey could sit there making jokes about bodies."

"It's only words to Casey. The words don't connect with anything real. It's a game," said Penn. "A game called 'Let's see Penn squirm.'"

"What happens when the police identify her?"

"I don't know. I wish I knew for sure how decomposed the body is. I suppose it depends on temperature, degree of exposure, and any number of other things. Obviously, it isn't the time for me to get a book about forensics on interlibrary loan."

"Oh, no," I murmured faintly. "Don't do that."

"What they can tell about the time of death

and the way she died is going to depend on the condition of the body." Penn wiped his mouth with the back of his hand. "Will you listen to me? I sound as cold-blooded as Casey."

"Her clothes," I said suddenly. "If her mother turned in a missing-person report—"

"She did," Penn interrupted.

"Don't those reports always begin, 'Last seen wearing . . .'?"

"Laurie had a ring," said Penn. He was staring at the road ahead. "I never thought of it until just now. I think maybe Bobby gave it to her." He frowned. "She didn't usually wear rings. It had something written inside the band. I'll have to ask Tessa."

"They're going to identify that body in no time," I said bleakly.

Four

When I got to school on Tuesday, I was stopped in the halls by Nikki Warren. Her eyes were bugging out with news. "Oh, my God, Joanna, have you heard? Laurie Jenkins is dead," she said. "They found her body."

I put my hand out to the locker suddenly to steady myself. Although I should have been prepared, I suppose on some level I had hoped this moment would never come—that the body would never be identified or that it would turn out to be someone else. "Penn's friend?" I gasped. "What happened? I thought she ran away."

"She must have come back. What does it matter? I guess she killed herself after all," Nikki said wildly. "Or maybe she was murdered. It's so awful! They found her up in the woods beyond Lookout Point."

"It must have been suicide," I said. "You told me she was depressed, didn't you?"

"Yeah, but why would she go up on a mountain to kill herself? It doesn't make sense. I bet some pervert murdered her and then dumped her body." Nikki's hoarse voice sank to a whisper. "And think—if that's what happened, then whoever did it is still running around loose!"

The floor seemed to shift under my feet as if I were on a pitching boat. She was talking about Penn and Stephen and Tessa.

"Are you okay?" cried Nikki, reaching out for me.

"I guess I'm still a little shaky. I had the flu, you know." I felt the cold metal of the locker between my shoulder blades as I sucked in air.

"Maybe you'd better sit down or something. I'm sorry to spring it on you like that. But you didn't even know her, so I didn't think you'd take it so hard." Nikki shook her head. "I guess now we may never know exactly what happened."

I certainly hope not, I thought.

"But when it's somebody you *know*!" Nikki cried. "It's so awful!"

"I'd better tell Penn."

"Of course," said Nikki, her eyes moist with sympathy. "It's going to be a terrible shock."

It was not until lunchtime that I saw Penn, and by then it was clear that the news had spread all over school. A couple of people I didn't know were standing by our table speaking to Tessa when I came up. They looked at me in a vaguely sympathetic way but left when I sat down.

Tessa's eyes were dark pools in her white face. "I've been telling people I was afraid something like this had happened, because I hadn't heard from Laurie," she said in a low voice.

"Has anybody seen Bobby today?" I asked.

"He must still be in D.C."

I had forgotten Bobby's trip to D.C. He had been going to look for Laurie. It seemed odd to think of that now.

Stephen pulled out a chair and sat down.

"You forgot your lunch," Tessa said quickly.

"How can you think about food at a time like this, Tess?" Stephen wiped sweat off his forehead with his palm.

"You'd better eat," she said. "You're going to get sick if you don't eat."

"This means the police are going to be

coming around again," said Stephen.

"It's been over two months since Laurie disappeared," whispered Tessa. "They can't expect us to remember every detail of what happened two months ago."

"Who else are they going talk to?" asked Stephen stubbornly. "We were the ones who knew her. We were her friends."

A strained silence fell.

Penn appeared at my side, looking white, as if he'd suffered a loss of blood. He wasn't carrying a tray. No one seemed to be eating.

"Where've you been?" Stephen asked. "I looked for you in calculus class."

"I just got to school a few minutes ago," Penn said. "Laurie's mother called my dad and told him they'd identified Laurie's body. He canceled his appointments and went right over. I thought I'd better go with him."

"What did they expect your dad to do?" asked Tessa.

"I think they wanted him to explain the pathologist's report."

For a moment we all held our breath. Finally Tessa spoke. "W-what did it say?" She and Stephen both had the habit of stuttering when they were rattled.

"Broken neck, broken ribs. Bad fractures—splintered bones, the kind you get from a really brutal blow. Dad kept telling Mrs. J. over and over again that Laurie didn't suffer."

"I expect that's true," said Tessa.

"Yeah, but I don't know how much of it Mrs. J. was taking in at that point," said Penn. "Dad phoned in a sedative for her. The drugstore delivered it, but as far as I could tell, it wasn't having too much effect."

"How long were you over there?" asked Stephen.

"Hours," said Penn.

"Jeez," said Stephen feelingly.

The chatter in the cafeteria around us sounded like monkeys at the zoo. The smell of burnt grease and spaghetti sauce made me feel ill.

"Yoo-hoo, sports fans!" Casey put down his tray and sat down. Grease and tomato sauce oozed from his sloppy joe. It trickled down the bun and gathered in glistening orange puddles on the plastic plate. "What'd you think of that calculus test, huh?" he asked.

"You've heard about Laurie, haven't you?" Tessa said in a warning tone.

"Yeah, sure," said Casey. "It's all over school."

"I think a subdued tone of voice would be more appropriate for the occasion, Casey dear," said Tessa. "Do you mind keeping a grip on your natural ebullience for once?"

"For pete's sake, the girl's been dead two months. What do you expect me to do? Cry?"

Tessa shielded her lips with one hand and mouthed a word to me: "Butthead."

I could see what she meant. Casey had a super-high IQ when it came to doing calculus problems or messing with computers. But when it came to ordinary common sense, he was an idiot.

Lunchtime lasted forever. Kids I didn't know stopped by the table to mutter clumsy words of condolence. I knew they were trying to be nice, but I was turned off by the obvious curiosity in their eyes.

After lunch Penn walked with me to class. "It must have been awful being with Laurie's mother," I said.

"It was no day at the beach," he said dryly. "A cop was there."

I glanced at him quickly. "Why didn't you mention that before?"

"I thought it was better not to—in front of Casey."

"Did the police ask you a lot of questions?"

"Naturally. He wanted to know everything I could tell him. Were there any guys in Laurie's life? Did she ever hitchhike? What about drugs? Did I remember seeing any suspicious people hanging around? Who were her friends? I was the one who had to talk to him. Mrs. J. wasn't much good to him. She had Laurie's old teddy bear and she kept hugging it and stroking it." Penn's eyes went blank, and I had to bend close to him to hear what he was saying. "You know, it was an awful thing I did, forging that letter from Laurie."

I grabbed his hand and held tight. "You panicked, that's all."

Penn shook his head. "I was so cold-blooded about it, as if I were working out a physics problem. It was a way to get the police off our backs—that's what I was thinking. But all this time, Laurie's mom has been thinking Laurie was in some kind of terrible trouble and she's been driving herself nuts asking herself where she went wrong as a mother." He glanced over at me. "Of course, she went wrong lots of places, but she didn't deserve this. I hardly recognized her. She's gotten so thin, she looks sick, and her hands were bony, like claws." He looked down miserably and scuffed the toe of his shoe in the dirt.

"You were only trying to protect Stephen and the others."

"Maybe, but it was selfish, too. I was trying to take the heat off before one of us cracked." He thrust his hands in his pockets. "It was cruel, that letter," he said, "and as it turns out, it was a waste. Now it's going to be worse than before. Laurie's not a missing person anymore."

Grass crunched under our shoes. We were standing on the lawn between the two classroom wings. Penn spoke quietly. "There was another reason Mrs. J. wanted my dad to come over. I didn't want to go into it in front of the others. After the police officer left, we were sitting around saying all these condolence-type things and I realized she was trying to get me out of the room. Finally she just out and out asked me to go in the kitchen and get them all some ice water. She wanted to ask dad if he could tell from the pathologist's report whether Laurie was pregnant."

"If you were in the kitchen, how did you know that?"

"Not from my dad telling me, that's for sure." Penn made a face. "I ran the water in the sink and then I went back and stood by the door and listened. I couldn't believe it. Here Laurie is dead, and Mrs. Jenkins is still fixated on whether she was pregnant."

I hesitated. "Was she?"

Penn gave me a look that said he was disappointed in me, and shook his head. "I never could understand how she got mixed up with Bobby in the first place. Talk about a mystery!"

"Bobby's not that bad."

"I don't know why you keep saying that," said Penn irritably. "He's subhuman. Seriously, don't you think that's weird about Mrs. J.?"

"Grief does strange things to people."

"It seemed like such a strange time to be wondering about Laurie's sex life."

"Penn, maybe you ought to go to the police right now and tell them the truth."

"Right," he said. "We'd all look real innocent, wouldn't we? We hid the body, concealed her death, forged a letter with her name on it. We'd come out looking like the junior achievement branch of Murder Incorporated. No, it's too late for that. Believe me, if I could do it, I would."

"Maybe it will blow over, like it did before," I said hopefully. "Maybe the police will go away when they don't find anything."

"Maybe. But right now I can only think of one bright spot. Mr. and Mrs. J. got so freaked out when the guy asked if Laurie had any men in her life—"

"Bobby," I said.

"Right. What with Mrs. J. shying as if she'd seen a snake at the sound of his name and Mr. J. puffing up in protection of his only chick, the whole Bobby question suddenly looked real juicy to the lieutenant. If you ask me, he was very interested to find out that Bobby was out of town. I could see him mentally counting up and figuring out that Bobby left the same day the body was discovered."

"Oh, no!"

Penn shrugged. "They're not going to get anything on Bobby. How could they? He didn't kill her. But it might help take the pressure off of us for a while. I don't have to tell you that would be a real help. You saw Stephen. He's hanging by a thread. And I'm really worried about Casey."

"Anything Casey could say would hurt him just as much as it would hurt any of you."

"I wish I were sure that he understands that," said Penn.

"What are we going to do?" I asked. "You

don't think the police—they didn't say anything that made you think they suspect you, did they?"

Penn's eyes were troubled. "I don't know. I just don't know."

After school let out, I sat in the living room and watched for Bobby. At five his mother came in from work and checked the mail. She's a big woman with broad, flat hips, and when she bent down to check the mailbox, her legs were squarely planted on the ground. Her movements were steady—she didn't look nervous. Maybe she didn't realize the police had started to wonder about Bobby. I couldn't be sure whether she had talked to Bobby's father or not. When people get a divorce, sometimes they don't speak after that. My mother and father, for instance.

My shoulders ached with tension, and the infernal video of Laurie's death ran over and over in my mind.

The house was quiet; my father was away. I had thrown open the front windows, hoping I would hear if Bobby's car drove up. The pond's bullfrogs boomed steadily, making a sound that seemed to well up from the ground, as if the earth itself were grumbling. The night breeze made the living-room draperies big-bellied, and at the back of the house a bedroom door slammed shut. My physics book lay on the coffee table, open to a wavy diagram of light frequencies. The page bent in the breeze, then flipped over, as if I were still at work on my physics. But I wasn't. I peered out the window, pressing my nose against the screen as if sheer anxiety could make Bobby appear. I couldn't have explained exactly why. Maybe all I wanted was an end to the painful suspense. It was three in the morning, but a dim square of light beside Bobby's front door showed that a lamp had been left on in the living room.

A motor hummed with the expectant rhythm of a repeated drumroll. Bobby! His car gleamed briefly under the streetlight, then abruptly bumped up into his driveway and stopped. A brief flash lit the car's interior when the door opened. I made out, just barely, a dark shape getting out. It was Bobby. He had come home. A long rectangle of light appeared over the threshold, then was obliterated by his shaggy shape. The door closed.

I turned away, breathing as heavily as if I had been running. A muffled crash sounded. Dead silence fell as the startled bullfrogs momentarily stopped their song. Holding my breath, I ran to the window. But there was no more noise from Bobby's, and in a few minutes the frogs resumed their gruff courtship. I might have thought I had imagined the crashing sound except that the dim square of light by the front door had disappeared. I wondered if Bobby had thrown the lamp. Hugging myself, I turned out the lights and scurried to my bed. There, with the covers pulled up to my chin, I listened to my heart flutter, panic-stricken and trapped under my ribs.

Five

I was waiting for Penn to show up when the phone rang. I picked it up.

"Joanna?" said Penn's voice. "I'm not going to be able to make it. The police have come by and they need to ask me some questions. I'm not sure how long it will take."

"Are you all right?" I inquired. I was gripping the receiver so tightly, my knuckles were white.

"Our plans for dinner are still on," he said calmly, not answering my question. "I should be by to pick you up at seven for sure."

"Okay. That's fine," I said. After I hung up, I stared at the phone for several minutes, unable to move. Once I had been stopped by a cop while driving through Raleigh. I remembered the looming blue figure close to my car window demanding to see my driver's license. "What did I do wrong, Officer?" I had asked over and over again. But he wouldn't answer. It turned out that my new license plate, which had been propped up in the back of the car window until I could get it screwed on properly, had fallen down. I didn't even get a ticket, but it took me hours to get over the scare. How much worse it must be for Penn, who had so much to hide!

"Aren't you going out with your friends anymore?" asked my father when he came home from work. He leafed through the mail.

"I'm meeting Penn and Casey for dinner," I said, stung by this reminder that my very presence made him feel crowded. I stuffed my diary in my book bag and headed for the door. "Actually, I'm on my way to the library."

I sat behind the steering wheel a moment, tears stinging my eyelids. I had to wait for my eyes to quit brimming so that I could see to drive. Every time I had almost persuaded myself that I didn't care what my father said, some petty rejection would remind me that he could still hurt me. I backed suddenly out of the driveway. It was a chilly day, and gusts of wind buffeted the car, but spring made itself noticed in pockets of color tucked here and there.

Daffodils bent low under the wind on a corner of our street, and in the sheltered crook of a white church someone had planted a triangle of scarlet tulips. Their cups full of sunshine, they glowed like Christmas-tree bulbs.

The library was a pseudocolonial structure surrounded by large trees that were just beginning to unfold their leaves. Inside, I sat down at one of the long tables and wrote in my diary.

. . . Why do I let my father get to me? I feel stupid when I burst into tears over some little thing he says. Maybe I overreact. But he makes me feel as if I'm in the way, as if I'm not worth the tiny bit of trouble I cause him. He's supposed to love me! I'm his daughter!

But it doesn't matter. I've got Penn. Only, what looked in the beginning like a beautiful love story is beginning to seem more like a sinister crime movie full of violence and lies. The nightmares, the shaky uncertain feeling whenever Casey makes a snide remark.

I've got to pull myself together. I can't afford to get morbid. So Penn has made some mistakes. Everybody makes mistakes. We'll get through this somehow. As long as we

*love each other, nothing else matters.
Nothing.*

"Hi." The sound of Penn's voice spun me around in my seat.

He put his hands on my shoulders. "Your father said you were here, so I came looking for you. I didn't want to wait until seven to see you. Is that okay? I'm not interrupting your work, am I?"

I rose and let my head rest against his chest. "No. It's fine," I said softly. "Hi."

"Let's get out of here," he said. "That gorgon at the front desk is giving us a nasty look." He hoisted my heavy book bag easily with one hand. and we went out to the cars. "Why don't we take your car home?" he said. "We don't want to have to come back here."

I drove back to my father's house, parked my car in the driveway, and got into Penn's car, which smelled strongly of peppermint. He ripped open a cellophane package and tossed one to me.

"So how was your talk with the police?" I asked, stuffing the peppermint in my mouth.

He shrugged. "Not too good."

"They don't suspect you!" I exclaimed.

"I don't know." He frowned. "They asked me if Laurie was acting normal before she disappeared. Well, she wasn't, so that was easy. But when they asked about what happened the day she disappeared, I started to sweat. I kept thinking of that typewriter I used to type the letter. It's back there in our garage."

"You didn't get rid of it?"

"No. Remember that nobody was thinking murder until they found her body. Hiding the body was so awful, I wasn't exactly dying to repeat the experience by dumping the typewriter. Also, I thought it would look pretty suspicious if anybody saw me pitching a typewriter into the river."

I was conscious of blood surging through my neck to my brain. "We could go get it now and get rid of it," I said.

"What if we're being watched?"

"You think the police are watching you?"

The sun was sinking low in the sky. Telephone poles cast bars of shadow across the road. A truck with an immense loaf of bread painted on its side rode past us.

"I don't know what I think," Penn said finally. "All I know is I can't face going back in the garage and grubbing under the tarp to find that typewriter. I'm afraid I'll come out with it and find myself nose to nose with a cop. All of a sudden they're everywhere. Do you think they need a search warrant to go into a garage?"

"I don't know. Have the police talked to the others yet?"

Penn shrugged. "I don't know. I couldn't reach Stephen or Tessa. We'll see them at dinner and we can find out then."

"I wonder if the police have talked to Casey."

"I can't let myself think about Casey," said Penn. "I'll go crazy if I do."

A car whizzed past blaring rap music.

"Casey's not stupid," I said. "He must see that anything he could say would implicate him."

Penn hesitated. "That's right, but I'm not sure that he understands that we've done things that we could be sent to prison for. In his eyes this is just a game. He thinks the only reason the rest of us are nervous is because we're sissies."

The restaurant, which was in the next town, was in a long, low, cement-block building. Its huge, ornate sign said *Omar Khayyam* in script. The patio in front was fenced in with scraggly rosebushes and featured a fountain lit with colored lights. It was the sort of glitzy place Casey liked, with waiters dressed in dinner jackets.

We found the others at a table by the front window. Stephen and Tessa stared gloomily out the window at the parking lot. Casey drained an oversized wineglass containing a liquid that resembled Pepto-Bismol. Three other glasses containing pink dregs were lined up on the table. Casey loved frozen strawberry daiquiris. Since he looked no older than about fourteen, restaurants wouldn't serve him alcohol, but he liked them just as well without the booze.

"Where've you guys been?" Casey peered at us over the top of his oversized menu. "Still being grilled by the police?"

"That was earlier," said Penn, pulling out a chair for me. "What about you?"

"I was superb," boasted Casey. "I don't think those guys are very bright." He folded the large menu, laid it down, and smirked.

"I don't know." Stephen shifted in his chair uncomfortably. "When they talked to me, I thought they seemed pretty sharp. They were awfully interested in the day Laurie disappeared."

"Well," said Tessa. "I'm sure we all pretty much agreed about what happened that day."

"Did they ask you about the ring?" asked Penn.

She nodded. "'Love, forever. B.' was engraved on the band. Laurie showed it to me. I told them that."

"That points right at Bobby," said Penn. He darted a quick glance around the table, waiting for us to agree.

"But that's not new, is it?" asked Tessa. "It's no secret that Laurie had hooked up with Bobby. Everybody knew it."

"Do you think the police knew it, though?" asked Stephen.

"Well, they've just got started," said Tessa. "Until now—" She hesitated and looked around at the others.

"Nobody was calling it murder," Penn finished for her.

"I guess they're bound to suspect him," said Tessa. "They always take a close look at the boyfriend."

"That's kind of rough on Bobby, isn't it?" said Stephen.

"I guess they're going to really go plowing around looking for every possible motive." Tessa heaved a sigh.

I suppose we were all thinking about the motives we had to hide. Except Casey.

"Heck, I don't know why you guys are so nervous," complained Casey. "As far as I can tell, they find women's bodies all the time and nothing ever comes of it. Why don't we order dinner, huh?"

"It said in the paper that the local police have an eighty-percent success rate in solving murders," put in Tessa.

"Yeah, but mostly that's because they come in and find the boyfriend standing over the body," said Casey scornfully. "Like I was saying, these guys are not too bright. Say, what do you think of this shirt?" He peered down at his own shirt front. "You don't think it's too much, do you? I wasn't quite sure about the yellow stripe with the lavender. Do you think it goes with the tie?"

"Very attractive," said Tessa. "Is it new?"

"Yeah." Casey grinned. "I liked the cut, so I got twenty, in different colors."

"You bought twenty shirts?" Stephen asked.

"Gift from Penn," said Casey. "It's nice. Makes a person feel appreciated. I mean, when a fellow does a favor for a fellow, he likes a little token of gratitude."

The waiter who had appeared at my elbow seemed mesmerized by this interchange. I saw his dark eyes darting from Casey to Penn. Clearly he was speculating wildly on what sort of favor would be worth a small fortune in shirts. "Are you ready to order?" he asked. "Or do you need a little more time?"

"Oh, we're ready, aren't we, gang?" said Casey. "I'll have the shrimp scampi, Caesar salad, and, for an appetizer, stuffed mushrooms. Yeah, I said I wasn't going to go overboard with these one-hundred-percent cotton thingies because of the ironing problem, you know? But then it hit me." He smiled broadly. "Tessa can help me out there."

Tessa, her face pink, stared resolutely down at the menu. "We're going to have the plain spaghetti, please, and bring two plates. We're going to share. We'll have water to drink."

Later Tessa and I found ourselves together in the ladies' room. It was painted lacquer red and had a vase of peacock feathers sitting in front of the vanity mirror. The paint on the wall behind it was peeling and the old mirror was wavy. Our images were so distorted that we looked frighteningly boneless and pale. Squinting into the mirror, Tessa smoothed her eyebrow with her pinkie.

"Can you believe Casey?" she asked. "He's getting worse and worse."

"Maybe it's a mistake to give in to him," I suggested.

Tessa pulled a comb violently through her hair. "It's because he can see we're nervous about the police," she said. "He thinks we'll give in to him on everything just to shut him up."

"That's blackmail."

"You're right," she said. "If it were just me, I'd tell him where to go. But you saw Stephen. He's white as a sheet. The police talked to him for two hours this afternoon. Two hours!"

"Why?"

"Who knows. And Stephen's not cool, like Penn. I expect he looked nervous. Naturally he would. He *is* nervous. And when a girl dies, they always figure a guy did it. When they talked to me, they were very curious about whether there were any guys in her life. What was Bobby like? Was he the jealous type? Did he have any good reason to be jealous? Was Laurie on drugs? Did she drink to excess? Of course, the truth is, Laurie was very straight, unless you figure in Bobby. I guess that's why the police are interested in him. Here is Laurie, who doesn't drink, do drugs, or even smoke, so it must be sex that was the problem. I think the police are basically puritans, don't you?"

"I haven't had a chance to form an opinion."

"I forget." Tessa stuffed the comb in her purse. "You're kind of a civilian in all this, aren't you?"

I shrugged. "Not really."

Tessa gave me a sudden sweet smile. "I know. You love Penn."

An elderly woman pushed open the door and stared at us a moment. I was afraid at first that she had heard what we were saying, but then I decided she was merely confused by the suddenly bright light of the ladies' room. She ducked into a stall.

When Tessa and I got back to the table, it had been cleared.

"Why do girls always go to the john in pairs?" asked Casey. "Guys don't ask for a date to go to the john. And girls take forever, too. What do you do in there?"

"We were throwing up," said Tessa tartly. "I'm not sure the food here is as fresh as it should be."

Casey, who had a tendency to be a hypochondriac, clutched his stomach in alarm.

Penn got up. "Let's get out of here."

It was dark outside now. Along the highway

points of light winked at us. A line of neon-colored drums marked highway construction, but Penn did not slacken his speed.

I asked him about the shirts.

"Casey had to have them." Penn sighed. "I mean, there we were in the middle of the mall, and he was having a temper tantrum. People were staring at us." He glanced at me. "Maybe he thinks they'll get him some girls."

"Huh," I said. "It's going to take more than a pretty shirt to get Casey any girl with half a brain." I reached over and touched Penn's arm. "Why do you give in to him? I'm not sure it's a good idea."

"I don't know whether it is or not. This is something I've got to play by ear."

"Casey's a blackmailer."

Penn thought about it. "You think?"

"Of course he is!"

"Look, Joanna, Casey doesn't want us to get arrested. What would he do if we got carried away to jail? We're the only friends he's got."

"If you're so certain of that, why do you let him run all over you?"

Penn looked uncomfortable. "I don't want to make him mad."

"You can't keep taking him to expensive

restaurants and spending a fortune on him," I cried. "It's an impossible situation."

"No." Penn sighed. "It's not impossible. I cashed in a big bond my grandmother gave me, so I've got some money right now. But I've got to be careful. All I need is for my dad to come across something like a receipt for a thousand dollars' worth of shirts. He'll figure I've gone out of my mind."

I sucked in my breath. "A thousand dollars! That much?"

"Yeah," he said somberly.

"You can't keep this up, Penn!"

He shrugged. "All I can do is take it a day at a time."

Six

❧

. . . A thousand dollars! Can't Penn see that by caving in to Casey he's digging himself into a hole he can't get out of? Fifty dollars for the broken record, hundreds of dollars a month spent taking Casey to glitzy restaurants, and now a thousand dollars' worth of shirts. It gets worse and worse. But it's not as if I can offer up a better idea. We can't afford for Casey to get mad at us and start talking to the police. He's sucking Penn dry, and there's nothing we can do about it.

As I approached the administration building the next morning, I heard an electric crackle and the disjointed, hollow sound of a voice on a car radio. A police car was in the circular drive that ran in front of the building; my stomach clutched when I spotted it. What were the police doing there?

I looked around wildly for a moment. Then, unable to stand the suspense, I walked into the office. A small woman stood at the long counter. Her stiff blond hair was like a nest of spun glass, and I could see glimpses of her scalp underneath. "May I help you?" she asked sweetly.

"Is it too late to order a yearbook?" I asked.

"You'll have to speak to the yearbook staff," she said. "I think the deadline for ordering is past, but they usually have some extra copies at the end of the year."

I glanced around the office. I could hear the hum and *clack* of a copy machine. "Who is the yearbook sponsor?" I asked, stalling for time. "I'm not sure how to get in touch with the staff."

"Mrs. Oldham does the yearbook. Wait a minute and I'll find her room number." She scuttled over to a wall chart and peered at it. "Two-oh-two Eastman," she said.

The door opened, and a massive man in a dark-blue police uniform stepped out of the principal's office. I found myself staring at the leather holster strapped to his hip. Close on his heels came Mr. Hansen, the principal; a second police officer; and Miss Tinker, a school counselor. Miss Tinker's white-blond hair was pulled back sternly in a fat bun, and she wore large black-rimmed bifocals. Her gaze fastened on me. "Here's one of Laurie's friends right here, Officer!" she said.

I glanced over my shoulder, hoping she was talking about someone else, but no one was standing behind me. "No!" I said too loudly. "I didn't even know Laurie."

Miss Tinker cocked her head at me as if she were a particularly intelligent parakeet. "There's nothing to be afraid of, my dear," she said. "These gentlemen just want to ask you a few questions."

"I never even met Laurie," I insisted.

Miss Tinker frowned. "I could have sworn . . . Don't I see you all the time with Penn Parrish? I was so sure you were one of that bunch."

"Yes," I said desperately, "but I moved here only a couple of months ago. Laurie had left before I even moved to town."

Miss Tinker turned away. "Anyway, Officer Callaway, you have her class schedule. I'm sure her teachers can give you a better idea of exactly who knew her."

Laurie had left before I even moved to town. My

words replayed in my mind sounding strangely
sinister, as if somehow my arrival had been the
cause of Laurie's disappearance. The bell rang,
and I was glad of an excuse to rush to homeroom.

As I took a seat in homeroom and glanced
around, a buzz animated the classroom. I was
uneasily aware that people were sneaking
glances at me. Although I hadn't known
Laurie, because of my friendship with the
group, I had become one of her mourners.
People were noticing me and pointing me out. I
tried not to let it bother me, but I could feel
my ears growing warm. Self-consciously I gazed
out the window. Blown by the wind, a sheet of
crumpled paper tumbled across the close-
shaven grass between the two classroom wings.
I knew that Bobby was assigned to my homeroom, and I had the uneasy feeling he might
appear suddenly, but there was no particular
reason to think he would. I wasn't sure why I
was so on edge.

After homeroom I was glad to move out into
the crowded, anonymous hallway. Now no one
would be staring at me. Feeling like a fugitive, I
went to my locker. I bent to get my books from
my locker, and a cloud of scent enveloped me.

Startled, I stood up and turned to face Koo Ambler.

"Ciao, lockermate," she drawled.

I hastily moved out of her way as she stepped forward. She kicked the locker wide open with the tip of her black boot. She wore studded black leather bracelets to match. Her face was pure white, and her black hair was gathered on top of her head and fell down in thin, ratty strings over her eyes. She bent to pick up one of the brown paper bags she kept at the bottom of our locker. The rear of her black leather skirt strained tight and reflected in white rectangles the light of the hall's high windows. She spoke, but her voice was muffled by the locker, and with the noise in the hall I couldn't quite make out what she said.

"What?" I asked.

She stood up and faced me. "Bobby's back. I talked to him last night. He's taking what happened to Laurie real hard."

I stared into her sooty eyes with fascination.

"He says if he gets hold of the guy who did it, he's going to kill him with his bare hands. And he's not kidding. He'll do it, too."

Why was she telling me this? I wondered if the hot guilt I felt showed on my face. It seemed important for me to say something. Anything. "Do the police have any leads?" I asked.

She shrugged. "Dunno. They came and got the letter from Laurie's mom, though."

"The letter?" I repeated stupidly.

"You know, the one she sent from D.C.," said Koo, tapping her boot. "They're sending it off to some lab. They're going over her room. They took her diary, her old letters—everything."

I licked my lips. "Sounds like they almost think it's somebody she knew."

Koo's dark brows drew together angrily. "Bobby didn't do it."

"Oh, I know!" I exclaimed. My certainty sounded too emphatic to my own ears, and I added, "I mean, I understand they were awfully close."

"Sure they were close. They were related, after all," snapped Koo.

I was surprised Koo took offense at my mild remark. I thought it was common knowledge that Bobby and Laurie were more to each other than family.

"Bobby says the police need proof," Koo went on, "but he doesn't. All he needs to know is who did it; then he's going to kill them. He wants them to suffer and die slow."

"I guess I'd better be getting on to class," I said.

All morning I kept imagining Bobby breaking Penn's legs or banging Stephen's head against concrete. He was savage, and in his mind they had it coming.

At lunchtime I was careful not to tell Tessa what Koo had said. Tessa already looked upset without any help from me. She sniffled and dabbed at her eyes as she mechanically unpacked bread, cheese, and two apples. Then she caught me looking at her. "Allergies," she said shortly. Around us heavy plastic dishes clattered, and our classmates shrieked in each other's ears.

"I saw a detective go into the teachers' lounge," Tessa said flatly. "He was wearing a dark suit, and he had a buzzcut. That's how I knew he was a cop and not a teacher."

"I wish I knew what the police were finding out." I glanced around me at the chaos of the cafeteria. At the next table sat a painfully skinny boy with black hair, a serious complexion problem, and a broad, rigid smile. To the amazement of his friends, he was blowing milk bubbles from his nose.

"The police aren't going to find out anything

from the teachers, that's for sure," said Tessa.

Stephen fell into a chair beside Tessa. "Talk about a morning from hell!" He looked pale and shaken.

"Have the police talked to you again?" Tessa asked quickly.

"Nah. Not today." He passed his hand over his forehead. "But it's all over school about Laurie. People are being so *nice* to me."

Instinctively Tessa reached for his hand.

"What were you talking to Koo about, Joanna?" he asked, turning to me suddenly. "I saw you two together."

"Koo's talked to Bobby," I admitted reluctantly.

"Bobby's back?" cried Tessa.

I nodded. "He got in night before last, really late. I think he must be over at Laurie's house, because I haven't seen him since he got back."

"What did Koo tell you?" asked Tessa. "I didn't know you and she even spoke."

"We don't. Not exactly. But she seemed to want to tell me that when Bobby finds out who killed Laurie, he is going to kill him with his bare hands."

A long silence fell.

"Why did she think you'd want to know that?" asked Stephen at last.

"I don't know. That's what worries me. Koo says even if the police need proof, Bobby doesn't. He can take the law into his own hands."

"That's civilized of him." Tessa fiercely tore off a bit of bread.

"I wonder why Koo singled you out to confide in," said Stephen.

"I have no idea. Maybe she knows I hang around with you guys and she figures you'd be interested. What worries me," I said, "is that I'm afraid Bobby's standards for proof aren't very high."

Trays clattered as kids tossed them onto the conveyor belt to the kitchen. The crash of the dishes and silverware punctuated the shrill din of the voices around us.

"You don't think Bobby's going to haul off and kill us on suspicion, do you?" asked Stephen after a moment.

Penn sat down. "Why are we talking about Bobby? Now there's a way to ruin lunch."

I filled him in on what Koo had said.

"I'm sorry I asked," Penn said.

"Where's Casey?" asked Tessa.

"Probably volunteering to have another interview with the police," said Stephen.

"He told me he enjoyed matching wits with

the police," said Tessa. "He's insane."

Penn made a face. "It's bad, all right. I wish Casey weren't so damn full of himself."

"I've had about all I can take of overpriced dinners with Casey," said Stephen.

"All for one and one for all," Tessa said, trying to sound positive. "We've got to do our share."

Penn rubbed his nose. "I'm taking him shopping this afternoon."

Silence greeted this announcement. We all knew Penn was in for an expensive afternoon.

Knowing that Penn was at some mall being bled dry by Casey made me restless and uneasy. After school I bought a magazine at the drugstore and took it to Hamburgers Galore. The bland cheerfulness of the fast-food restaurant was soothing, and I began to feel better. The magazine was full of soft-focus photographs of roses and beautiful models in wide-brimmed white hats. I wished I could step into its pages.

The banquette seat shook and I looked up, startled. A blunt, hairy hand was on the backrest right beside me. My gaze traveled up the brawny arm to Bobby's face. "Hey," he said hoarsely.

"Hi," I gulped.

He put a Styrofoam coffee cup on the table

and sat down across from me. The booth trembled with his weight. "I guess you heard about Laurie," he said.

"Yes. I'm so sorry."

"All this time I thought she was mad at me. I thought I'd done something wrong." His eyes were hurt and puzzled. "But now it makes sense."

"What makes sense?" I whispered.

"Why I didn't hear from her." His Adam's apple moved convulsively. "She didn't call me because she couldn't."

I couldn't think what to say and watched him helplessly.

"You don't think there could be some mistake, do you?" he asked thinly.

"What?" Remembering Bobby's threats, I was so frightened, it was hard to concentrate.

"I mean, like, maybe it wasn't her after all. Maybe it's somebody who switched clothes with her and stole her ring."

Two of Bobby's middle fingers had scraped knuckles—probably from belting somebody—and my breath came in short gasps as I looked at his blunt fingers spread out on the table next to his cup.

. . . *Sitting there at Hamburgers Galore, I felt sorry for Bobby, and when I thought*

about how I would feel if Penn's body had
been found rotting in the woods, I wanted to
put my arms around him and comfort him.
But I couldn't. I couldn't even touch him, I
was so afraid of him. It was like sitting next
to a keg of dynamite and watching the fuse
burn. When he got up suddenly and left, I
felt dizzy with relief.

Whatever happens, I have to keep Bobby
from finding out the truth.

Seven

Dear Diary,
   We have to go to Laurie's memorial service, all of us. I keep worrying that one of us is going to stand up right in the middle of the service and confess everything. I know it's crazy, but that's what keeps going through my mind. Hanging by a thread—wasn't that what Penn said? It's true! It seems as if almost anything might go wrong. . . .

The memorial service for Laurie was at Brenner's Funeral Home across from the shopping mall.

"I wonder if this means the police have the body," Penn said. "I mean, isn't that the main difference between a funeral and a memorial service? No body?"

The parking lot of the funeral home was enclosed with a low brick wall that separated it from the veterinarian's office next door. A hearse and two shiny black limousines were at the back of the brick building. When I climbed out of the car, I could hear the yipping of the dogs at the vet's boarding kennel.

"Maybe there's no body for the funeral because they're still examining it. Maybe they're doing more tests at the state lab," Penn went on in a low voice.

"Maybe Laurie's folks don't like the idea of having a coffin up there," I said, trying to sound calm. "Maybe that's why they prefer a memorial service. It might not have anything to do with what the police are doing."

The funeral home turned out to be a dizzying succession of small living rooms, each grandly furnished with plush sofas and wing chairs upholstered in lime green or blue. "We're here for the Jenkins—" Penn began. A tall man in a suit gravely swung both his arms to the right, as if he were about to tap-dance. Penn took the hint and veered to the right down a short hall. We filed into a long room that was filled with wooden pews. A railing stretched across the front where the altar should have been, and behind the railing on an easel stood a large, heavily retouched photograph of Laurie that made her look like a plastic doll. The photograph was flanked by triangular bouquets of pink flowers perched on wire stands.

"That's her senior picture," whispered Penn.

We were conscious of the rustling and low murmurs behind us as mourners came in. The place was already almost full. Stephen stumbled down the aisle, looking terrified. He and Tessa slid in next to us. "Isn't this place awful?" Stephen said under his breath. "It's like a church but it's not really a church, you know?"

Belatedly I realized that a different congregation sat in the shadows in a dark room to the right of the railing. I couldn't make out any one face, but I knew Bobby must be in that dark room with the rest of the family.

To me the service seemed colorless, a homogeneous, fast-food version of a funeral. Music swelled from an invisible organ. Several people came up front and spoke, one after the other, but nothing they said seemed to have much relevance either to Laurie or to her death. The first

speaker seized the opportunity to give a short
sermon encouraging everyone to follow the example of Jesus. The second speaker, a stout man
with a small Kiwanis button on his lapel, gave a
brief, entirely fictional account of the wonderful
home Laurie's parents had provided for her. The
final speaker was a woman who had been
Laurie's troop leader in Brownies. "Laurie always
tried," she said. "Whether it was building a camp
fire or selling cookies, she always did her very
best." She concluded with a tearful rendition of
the Scout's oath.

I glanced around me, wondering if anyone
else thought this was as stupid as I did.
Evidently not. Some people had been moved to
tears.

The invisible electric organ swelled again,
and we all stood and filed slowly out a door to
the left of the railing. The door opened onto a
small, dark, windowless room that was crowded
and confused. The Brownie woman sobbed into
a handkerchief. Near her was a woman in a
black dress who had flyaway hair like Laurie's.
Her cheeks were darkly shadowed and her eyes
were blank. I watched Penn shake her hand and
say something to her. Then, as if he were at a
cotillion, he moved smartly in two steps over to

a large, florid man and shook his hand as well. I
lost sight of him for a moment in the crush, but
then I felt his hand fold over mine. "I think we
can go now," he said. Beads of sweat glistened
on his upper lip. We made our way through the
crowd and gratefully stepped outside. A dog
yipped.

"Where's Stephen?" asked Penn agitatedly.
"Did you see whether Casey ever showed up? He
should have been there."

"It doesn't matter," I said. "Let's go."

"Stephen looked terrible," he said, as we
drove away.

As we passed the clock outside First Union
Bank, it blinked 7:32. It was 63 degrees.

"That was truly awful," I said.

"They should have had a priest or a minister."
Penn licked his lips. "Talk about an argument for
organized religion—where did they dig up those
speakers? None of them even seemed to know
Laurie."

"I'm glad they didn't ask any of you to speak,
though," I said.

Penn stared at me. "You're right. I hadn't
thought about that. It could have been worse."

The entire school was speculating about

how Laurie died. Occasionally I heard fragments of sentences about perverts or serial
killers, and once I heard somebody talking
about something they'd seen on *America's Most
Wanted*. But for the most part, gruesome con-
versations died out if any of us approached.
Then an article on Laurie's death appeared in
the *Evening Telegram*.

VICTIM'S LETTER FORGED, POLICE SAY

Police investigating the death of Laurie
Jenkins, the Barton City teenager whose
body was discovered last week in woods
three miles north of Lookout Point,
say Jenkins may have died shortly after her
January 13 disappearance. Although Alva
Jenkins, her mother, received a letter pur-
porting to be from Laurie on January 26,
police say preliminary lab reports indicate
the letter was a forgery. Laboratory analysis
showed that the signature was an inked-in
carbon copy of Jenkins's signature. Police
declined to speculate who could have per-
petrated the hoax or what connection, if
any, the letter had with Jenkins's death.
"Obviously, whoever wrote the letter had

access to a copy of Laurie Jenkins's signature," said Lieutenant John Davies. "I can make no further comment at this time."
The police investigation is continuing.

"We're in for it now," said Penn gloomily when I ran into him in the parking lot. "I guess I should have seen it coming."

Penn was right. The atmosphere at school changed suddenly. The following week the glances that came my way seemed charged with hostility. Nikki Warren spoke to me bluntly. She was the sort who was always telling people "something for their own good."

"Somebody who knew her wrote the letter," she told me. "It stands to reason. And you guys knew her."

"I didn't," I protested.

"Not you, personally, maybe," she allowed, "but Penn and all the rest of them were her closest friends. Everybody figures they must have faked that letter. Who else had her signature?"

"That doesn't make sense," I protested. "Why would they have her signature any more than anybody else? It's not as if people write letters to their friends at school."

"Yeah, but they'd know how to get her signature if they wanted," she insisted.

I made an incoherent protest, but she went on.

"And why would her friends forge the letter?" Nikki asked patiently. "Because they must have killed her, that's why."

I froze, shocked by her plain words.

She leaned toward me, her tiny gold ear studs glittering. "Tell me honestly, Joanna. Haven't you seen signs those guys are into satanic-cult stuff?"

"No!" I choked with sudden hysterical giggles.

Nikki tilted her head. "That's what people are saying, you know," she said earnestly. "That maybe Laurie was a sacrifice in some ceremony-type thing or something."

"You can't believe that! It's ridiculous!"

"I keep an open mind," said Nikki piously. "All I'm telling you is that's what people are saying."

I was anxious to get away from her. Bizarre though her ideas about the crime were, she was too close to the truth for comfort.

That afternoon Penn and I stood by his car in the parking lot. I was tired, and I was finding it hard to ignore the looks we were getting. "It's awful," I said. "People are acting as if we're criminals."

"I am a criminal," said Penn bleakly. "I've got to get rid of that typewriter."

I looked up at him. Cars were speeding out of the lot, spewing exhaust fumes. Around us kids called to one another, their voices straining over the roar of the motors—yet we were as alone as if we had been in the desert. "I'll go with you," I said.

"I guess you have to," he said with a faint smile. "I need your car."

The Corvette stood out too much to be suitable for ditching the typewriter. I knew that. It was the sort of car people remembered.

"Do you still think the police might be watching your house?" I asked.

"Sure. It's possible. But I've got to take the chance. If the cops go in the garage and throw back that tarp . . . they'll have enough evidence to charge me with murder. I can't sit around and wait for that to happen."

"But you didn't do it!" I cried. "Stephen wouldn't let them charge you with murder."

"Maybe." His hand rested lightly on my hip. "Maybe not." I could see blue veins bulging on the back of his hand, and the sun-bleached fine hairs white against his lightly freckled skin. "I'm an accessory for sure, though," he said. "And if they find that typewriter, they've got me."

"Are you going to do it tonight?" My gaze flew to his face.

"Yeah. I'll come by and get you at eight unless there's some good reason not to—like, if the cops are at my house."

I nodded mutely.

Eight

Penn's car pulled up in my driveway at eight. My father peeked out the window. "Here comes the boyfriend," he said. He glanced at me. "Is that what you're going to wear on your date? You look like a cat burglar."

I jumped guiltily. I had dressed in black jeans, black turtleneck, black socks and shoes. "It's comfortable," I said shortly.

Outside, the night air was chill and clear. The streetlight, gleaming coldly behind a tree, cast long ominous shadows. Penn was wearing dark clothes, and his pale face and fair hair seemed to float in the shadows. When I drew closer to him, I realized he was breathing hard. I stumbled into his arms, and he gave a low chuckle. "We must look like two shadows," he said softly. "Black on black."

Blood was pounding in my veins. Penn pressed his lips to mine, and I was startled that his lips were cold. We clung together, and when he kissed my neck, I nuzzled my face in his hair. The smell of his hair was faint, familiar, and completely intoxicating.

His breath tickled my neck, and I felt his open mouth fasten on the soft flesh of my neck. "Mmm," I murmured.

"I love you," he said thickly.

I pulled away from him. "Did you see anyone when you left the house?" I asked.

He shook his head. "No. But maybe the cops are disguised as bushes."

"Don't joke about it," I pleaded.

"I'm not laughing, am I?" he asked softly. "We can drive to the post office and leave my car there."

I closed my eyes. "We better move the typewriter from your car to mine right here. What if somebody sees us doing it at the post office?"

Penn shivered. "Do it right here? With Bobby across the street watching our every move? No way."

We got in separate cars without another word, and I followed Penn downtown. When we arrived at the post office, I saw the logic of his choice. Shopping centers and fast-food restaurants would be full of potential witnesses at this time of night—cruising kids, nighttime shoppers, and people going out for frozen yogurt. An extremely desolate place like the city dump had its own risks, because we had no reason for being there at night. But the post office was near perfect. A few box holders did venture there to check their mail after dark, and we might pass as having legitimate business.

The post office was ablaze with light; the rental mailboxes were lit up behind glass windows as if in a display case. An olive-green mail truck rolled out on the street. The traffic light changed from red to green, and the truck rumbled away into the night. Penn parked under a large tree at the corner of the lot. When we got out, the tree loomed huge and dark over us, blotting out the sky. A dark figure passed us, walking on the sidewalk, hands thrust into pockets, knit cap pulled over ears. I darted an anxious look at the Corvette. At least in the gloom under the tree, it was hard to see Penn's car. Its trunk flew open and Penn lifted out a cardboard box that said GEORGIA PEACHES. Then he hoisted the box into my car and slammed the trunk closed.

"Let's go," he said, sliding in next to me.

I was a nervous driver, and when I hesitated at the light, I could feel Penn's tension rising. "Let me drive," he said abruptly.

"You'd better not." I knew he was almost incapable of driving under the speed limit.

Perhaps he realized that, too, because he didn't argue. His fingers gripped the armrest. "Go out Old Carriage Road," he said. "There's a bridge over the river, but nobody lives out there."

I saw a sign: BRIDGE ICES BEFORE ROAD. Unexpectedly, the lights of a small square house loomed almost directly ahead of us. I could make out a gallowslike outline in the backyard, silhouetted against the night sky. A swing set, I supposed. "Damn," said Penn. "I guess I haven't been out on this road in a while. They must have just built the place."

I drove past the silent house and out onto the bridge. I cut off my car lights but left the motor running. My heart thumped wildly as Penn slid open the door. In the rearview mirror, I saw his dark form move around the car, and then—blackness. I turned around. The trunk was up. I could no longer see the lighted house. There was a splash, and a moment later he slipped back into the passenger seat, breathing hard. "Drive," he said. My heart was in my mouth as I stepped on the accelerator. "Now turn your lights back on," said Penn.

I glanced behind me. "The trunk is still open."

"Don't worry about that now," he snapped. "We'll close it in a minute."

Wind ruffled my hair and the car was cold. I glanced over. "Penn! Shut the door!" I cried.

"Drive a couple of more minutes and then we'll pull off the road and do it. I don't want to make any noise so close to the house."

The road was heavily wooded on both sides. In only a couple of minutes the lights of the small house by the river had disappeared from my side mirror. I stopped the car but didn't pull off for fear of getting stuck on the weed-covered shoulder. Penn leapt out and the car rocked as he slammed the trunk shut. Then he got back in and shut his door. "Let's go," he said.

We drove for some minutes in silence. "Turn left onto Forty-three, now," he said.

"You don't think anybody saw you, do you?" I asked.

"I didn't notice anybody when I left the house," Penn said. "And if somebody had been tailing us, we'd have seen them behind us. It's not as if there's any traffic on these country roads. We would have spotted a police car. I think we're okay. If the people in the house heard the splash, it'll pass for an animal noise of some kind. That's why I didn't want to shut the trunk or the car door. If they heard the car noises together with the splash, they might make the connection and realize somebody had dumped something off the bridge."

"The police can't be watching you," I said. "They probably don't have the manpower to stake out the houses of everybody who knew Laurie."

Penn's teeth flashed white in the dark. "Trying to convince yourself?"

"Yes," I said honestly.

. . . I think I'm losing it. I was walking across the grass from Eastman to the cafeteria when I heard the flapping of wings. I couldn't stop myself from jumping at the sound. A shadow moved on the grass, and I looked up to see a crow overhead, its beak glistening in the sunlight. A harsh warning caw ruffled the feathers on its throat. It wheeled in a semicircle and

finally landed high on the cafeteria.
Could this be a bad omen, Diary?

At lunch Tessa was waiting at our usual cafeteria table. I pulled out a chair and sat down. "You won't believe what Stacy Creech told me," Tessa blurted. "She said everybody thinks that somebody who knew Laurie must have written that letter, but she knows it couldn't have been us because we were her friends and we didn't have any reason to want her dead!"

Around our table conversation continued in shrieks and cackles, as if a circus were going on with horrible painted clowns grimacing and pretending to laugh.

"It was nice of her to say she didn't suspect us," I said.

"Why *should* anybody suspect us? We didn't have any reason to kill Laurie!" cried Tessa.

Silence lay between us. We both knew that was a lie.

"Did you have any idea that people were saying we had written that letter?" asked Tessa.

I admitted I had heard that.

"Anybody could have written it," said Tessa, agitated. "All they would have needed was Laurie's signature."

It occurred to me that as isolated as I was from gossip at school, Tessa was even more out of it. I was amazed that she could have fooled herself that no suspicion was attached to us.

"Last year when Laurie was on the annual staff, she signed the final page along with the rest of the staff, and a thousand copies of the annual were printed up!" Tessa said shrilly. "Anybody could have gotten hold of a copy."

I knew there was no point in trying to reason with her. She ran her hand through her dark hair several times. "Maybe I should write a letter to the school paper. We can't let these rumors go on."

Stephen sat down. "So, how do we like being suspects?" He squeezed Tessa's hand.

"We hate it," she said passionately.

"It can't hurt us," he said. "They're not putting anybody in prison yet on rumors."

At least the typewriter was at the bottom of the river, I thought. The police could not tie Penn to the forged letter.

    . . . I wanted to tell Stephen and Tessa that we had gotten rid of the typewriter, but I wasn't sure I could bring myself to speak of it. The whispered asides, the strange glances

when I walk into the classroom, seem different to me now. My bones feel the chill of those cold looks. It must be that guilt is weighing on me. I guess I'm shaken. I'm an accessory to a crime now, and maybe it's hit me that there's no going back.

I've got to stay calm. I had no choice but to help Penn. If he got sent to jail, I don't know what I would do. The big thing is that the police can't pin Laurie's death on us unless they come up with a good motive. . . .

Casey has got to keep his mouth shut! If he lets on that he's been breaking into computers, the police will have all they need. No matter what—we can't let that happen!

Nine

VICTIM BEATEN, SAY POLICE

Police say murder victim Laurie Jenkins, 17, was savagely beaten and may have died of injuries from the beating. Preliminary autopsy reports, say police, show Jenkins suffered a broken neck and two broken ribs in the fatal attack. She had been struck with such force that the bones were splintered. "This was a savage crime," said Officer James Higgins. "We are asking any witnesses who saw a vehicle in the Lookout Point area on or around January 13 to come forward. Anyone with information that may be helpful should contact the police."

*   *   *

As I sat at the kitchen table after school, I had the eerie sensation that I was reading about an entirely different crime. Laurie hadn't been beaten—she had fallen to her death. My first impulse was to call Penn, but we had agreed we could not talk freely on the phone, in case Penn's line was tapped. I sat on the living-room couch and read every word of the paper over again— SPELLING BEE CHAMPION GOES TO WASHINGTON; SCHOOL BOND REJECTED; RECIPE WINNERS FETED. The innocent doings of ordinary people seemed so distant, I might have been reading about the customs of some tribe in the Amazon. All I could think about was the police investigation. Even though I knew the paper would shed no more light on it, I kept reading it over and over as if I could somehow squeeze out more information.

I was staring at the social column—a lingerie shower was hosted by Arrington Todd and Maybelle Williams at the home of Marjorie Simpson—when I heard Penn drive up. I ran out to meet him and was at the car door before he had even gotten out. I slid in next to him. "Have you seen the paper?"

He nodded. "The body must have been pretty badly decomposed by the time it was found. I suppose there's no way to tell what kind of blow has broken a bone, really. That's why we hear so much about the famous 'blunt instrument.' But you would think lab analysis would show she had fallen."

"Obviously not," I said.

The newspaper article had an electric effect on the school. Suddenly nobody suspected us—everyone suspected Bobby, instead. In physics class, kids behind me were talking about him. "He threw Neil over the railing, remember? It was a miracle he didn't break his back."

"Casey told me he hit a kid on the head with a brick when he was only in the first grade! Maybe he's one of those weird genetic freaks. You know, that screwy stuff with chromosomes that's supposed to make guys into tall skinny murderers?"

"Bobby isn't skinny," someone pointed out.

"Maybe he was jealous," somebody said.

"It's always the boyfriend," said a squeaky voice.

"If Miss Timmons will deign to give me her attention, I will endeavor to explain problem number six," said Mr. Dockerty sarcastically.

The voices behind me abruptly stopped.

Dockerty's chalk scratched on the green chalkboard. A breeze ruffled the papers on his desk. Dockerty had a fanatic's belief in fresh air and had thrown the windows open, though the skies outside were dark and the breeze was chill. I gathered my sweater close around me and tried to concentrate, but the chalk marks on the board seemed to move and rearrange themselves into nonsense.

The weather had turned blustery. Daffodils in front of the administration building, whipped by violent buffets, were tattered. The rushing air stung my cheeks but filled me with a strange exultation, so great was the relief of having suspicion fasten suddenly on Bobby. Squinting, I made my way, half-blinded by the wind, toward the parking lot. Then, rounding the corner of the building, I blundered into Bobby.

I was stunned to come on him so suddenly, just when everyone had been talking about him. He threw his arms around me and held me tightly in his grip. Looking up at him, I was surprised to see that tears streaked his reddened face. His hair blew unheeded across his face. "I loved Laurie," he said in a choked voice. "I never would have hurt her! You believe me, don't you, Joanna?"

I nodded vigorously as I struggled to get my breath.

"I loved her more than anything." He lifted his chin and let out a loud, incoherent cry of pain. Belatedly I realized he had let me go.

"Don't pay any attention to what people are saying, Bobby," I gasped. "It doesn't mean a thing."

"Just wait till I get my hands on the guy who did it," he growled. "I'll make him pay. I'll start with his fingers and break every bone."

I sucked in air; then, realizing after some seconds that I had forgotten to breath, I exhaled in a puff. Suddenly I had to get away. I felt sick. Not standing on ceremony, I bolted for my car. But Bobby, his face screwed up into a glower, blocked my way. "What gives? What do you care what I do to the guy who killed Laurie?"

I pressed my fingers to my lips a moment. "I can't stand it when you talk that way," I cried. I realized I had made a mistake to try to run from him. Maybe I had even made him suspicious. "It scares me," I gasped. "You sound like some kind of animal."

His face darkened. "The guy that murdered Laurie—there's the animal."

"I've got to go, Bobby. I have to get on home."

"I'm not stopping you," he growled, stepping aside.

I felt his gaze boring into my back as I hurried to my car.

Driving away, I licked my dry lips. Maybe Bobby would crash his car, I thought with an absurd flicker of hope. He looked in no shape to negotiate traffic. Then I wouldn't have to be afraid of him anymore. I shivered. Penn's red car appeared in my rearview mirror. He waved, then gestured in the direction of Evergreen Street. A few minutes later we converged in The Bakery parking lot.

The blue spires of the herblike plants by the steps were whipping in the breeze. A crumpled piece of paper scudded noisily past my feet.

"Did I see you hugging Bobby Jenkins," Penn asked, "or am I having hallucinations?"

"Don't be silly." I was alarmed to see Penn's face had grown still and became a waxen mask. "He was the one who hugged me!" I protested. "He's going crazy about all these rumors that he beat Laurie to death."

Penn looked away from me toward the dusty windows of The Bakery. Taped to the door, notices advertising plays and garage sales crackled in the breeze. The wind scoured the pebbled parking lot. "Maybe I'm going crazy," he said softly.

For a second I was afraid to move toward him, but he took a step toward me and enfolded me in his arms. "I kept remembering how you said Bobby wasn't so bad," he said. "I couldn't stand it if you left me. You're all I've got."

I pressed my icy nose against his chin. "Hey, I'm not going anywhere."

He laughed unsteadily. "This is all pretty insane, isn't it?"

"If you think I'm in love with Bobby," I said, "then that is insane." I hesitated. "He terrifies me."

Penn laughed. "You and Stephen both. Stephen's even started carrying that pistol around. Let's go inside. It's freezing out here."

He put a hand at my waist and piloted me into The Bakery. The smell of warm bread and spices was comforting. We went through the line, collecting cookies and steaming mugs of hot chocolate.

We took a table in the corner, where the windows met, and looked out on the gloom of the street and the parking lot. A station wagon covered with bumper stickers parked in front of the feed store. SAVE THE WHALES. SAVE THE SEALS. I BRAKE FOR ANIMALS. VOTE VEGETARIAN.

"What did you mean," I said, "when you said Stephen is walking around with a gun?"

"That old pistol he brought to the cabin for target practice. He's carrying it everywhere."

"If he takes it to school, he could get in a lot of trouble."

"Maybe. But he's worried about Bobby." Penn winced. "Jeez, this is all we need. Here comes Casey."

Casey's ancient car bumped into the parking lot.

He pushed the glass door open and a cold wind swept my napkin off the table.

"Wow!" he cried. "Ho-ho, pals of mine. Great to run into you! Why didn't you say you were going to The Bakery?" He sprawled on a chair at our table, knees apart, and grinned broadly. "That hot chocolate sure looks good, Joanna. But I like mine with lots of whipped cream and those itty-bitty bits of chocolate." He turned expectantly toward Penn.

Penn opened his mouth as if to speak, then abruptly closed it and stood up. "With whipped cream?" he asked.

. . . Casey is the most conceited boy I've ever met. And why shouldn't he be? He has

all of us dancing to his tune. When he treats
Penn like his slave, I feel hot anger rising
from my throat like a bad taste. I feel blood
vessels expanding in my head, and I have to
bite my lip to stop myself from telling him
off. . . .

Penn placed the hot chocolate on the table
and sat down. Casey lifted a heaping teaspoon of
whipped cream and slurped it noisily.

The door opened suddenly, and Tessa and
Stephen came in. "Hello, all!" cried Tessa. Her
cheeks were bright pink from the chill wind and
her eyes were unnaturally bright. She came over
to our table, sat down, stripped off her jacket,
and draped it on the back of the chair.

I couldn't stop myself from glancing anxiously at Stephen, who had gone up to the
counter. He was reaching for chocolate-chip
cookies. He habitually wore such baggy pants
and shirts that he could have hidden a bazooka,
nevermind a single pistol.

"You know something, Joanna?" Casey
smirked. "I just happened to be at the library,
and I checked the Raleigh phone book, and
there wasn't a single Rigsby listed. I thought
you said your mother lived in Raleigh? Now,

why would anyone lie about something like that?"

I stared at him, speechless. I felt like a deer caught in headlights. The silence seemed to last an eternity, but it must have been only a couple of seconds before Tessa said impatiently, "Don't be stupid, Casey. Lots of people have unlisted numbers these days." She stared directly at him. "If you keep drinking hot chocolate every day, you are going to get F-A-T. Of course, we will love you just the same, won't we, Joanna?"

> *Dear Diary,*
>
> *I hate Casey. I don't think it had quite added up to that before—all his petty insults and malicious digs. But now I realize Casey is evil. He is one of our group, but he isn't on our side. He is our enemy.*
>
> *At school, the spotlight has shifted off us and onto Bobby. I feel guilty for being glad about that, but I can't help myself. While that searchlight of suspicion was on Penn, I couldn't stand it. I love him so much, I wouldn't know what to do if anything happened to him.*
>
> *Now it looks like he'll be all right. We*

could breathe easy if we didn't have to worry about Casey! But we can't have any peace. He's gnawing away at us, eating us alive.

I really do hate him!

Ten

On Saturday morning Penn and I arrived at the cabin early. Stephen and Tessa got there a few minutes after us. Mist floated over the river and shrouded the trees, giving the familiar scene an eerie look. Although we'd often walked in the woods around the cabin, this morning they were mysterious, as if they hid werewolves.

Inside, it was dark enough that we had to switch on the lights. The lamp cast a warm glow on the pink roses of the chintz-covered couch. Soon Tessa was standing at the kitchen counter. Her dark hair fell unheeded over her eyes as she sifted flour. She was singing a sad song to herself, but I couldn't make out the words.

"We ought to be hearing from colleges pretty soon," said Stephen. "Did you realize that?"

117

"Not until April fifteenth," said Tessa.

"They always say the fifteenth," said Stephen, "but last year people started hearing around the eighth."

"Let's not talk about that now," said Tessa. "It's so peaceful here." She gazed out the window. A small brown wren burst into song.

"I wonder if Casey will get into MIT," I said. They all looked at me in sudden alarm, and I realized with dismay that Casey's name had broken the quiet of the moment. We had all been calm and relaxed. I had ruined that by mentioning him.

"I expect he'll get into MIT okay," said Penn. "Though there's no telling. Remember Richard Totten, last year? Fourteen hundred on the SATs, president of the senior class, played every sport known to man, and still he got wait-listed at Dartmouth."

A litany followed in which everyone contributed the name and sterling credentials of some unfortunate who had been turned down by his or her first-choice school.

"Fifteen hundred on the SATs," said Tessa, "a nationally ranked swimmer, and he didn't get into West Point."

Stephen sighed. "Can't we talk about something else? I'm sorry I brought it up."

"I shouldn't have mentioned Casey," I said remorsefully. "His name is poison."

Penn was sprawled in a chair, his legs draped carelessly over its arm. I remembered how his air of ease had enchanted me the first time I saw him. "It's not that bad," he said.

"Hah!" snorted Stephen. "Sure, it's that bad. Don't try to tell me that Casey's a good guy. You know what came for me in the mail yesterday? One of those pamphlets that list the warning signs of mental illness! No return address, but guess whose handwriting? He'd run yellow Hi-Liter all over symptom number six, 'Do you have uncontrollable outbursts of temper?' And there I was, opening it with my mom peeking over my shoulder asking who had written me!"

"Casey may try to get at us," said Penn, "but I can't believe he'd give us away to the police."

"I wish I could be sure of that," said Stephen.

"If we only knew what the police were up to!" cried Tessa. "That's what's so awful—not knowing. If we could keep track of how the investigation was going, we could relax."

"Or maybe we'd be even more nervous," suggested Stephen.

"If somebody saw our cars up at the park, I

think they'd have come forward by now," said Penn.

"Nobody saw us," said Stephen. "Remember what time of year it was. Nobody but us would be insane enough to try a picnic in January. Besides, it was months ago. Nobody sits around saying, 'Hey, honey, wasn't it May seventh when I saw that blue Chevy on Sunset Avenue?'"

A silence fell over us. Perhaps the others were thinking, as I was, that Laurie had died on the thirteenth, an easy date to remember. "Unlucky thirteen," Penn had called it. And though Stephen's Chevy might be forgettable, Penn's red Corvette was a different matter.

Tessa rinsed her hands and dried them on her shirt. "I keep remembering that Casey didn't have anything to do with writing that letter to Laurie's mom. He didn't help hide the body, either. That's why he's so cool. He probably thinks he's not in deep, and that even if we got caught, they would let him off easy. For all we know, he's playing with the idea of turning state's evidence."

"I don't think so," said Penn. "You'll notice he's always careful not to say anything in front of Joanna."

"It's lucky he doesn't realize Joanna knows

everything," said Stephen. "There'd be no stopping him. He'd be setting up reenactments of Laurie's death, telling us about how many poor suckers are on death row, building model electric chairs, and showing us how they work. When I think how bad he is now, I hate to think what he'd be like if he let himself go."

"I don't think he'll do anything that would foul up getting into MIT," put in Penn. "He wants that."

"But would it hurt him?" argued Stephen. "He'd be cooperating with the police."

"Sure it would hurt him," said Tessa. "If we're guilty, then he's an accomplice."

"The point I'm making is," said Penn, "Casey's got a little bit of self-control. He's not going to go to the cops."

"He must know that if he did, I'd do my very best to bring him down with us," said Stephen savagely. "I swear I'd follow him all the way to hell."

A car door slammed and our faces turned toward the door as if on a single string. Casey burst in. "Banzai, buckeroos!" he cried. He tossed a bulging black plastic bag on the floor. "I brought shirts for Tessa to iron," he cried. "You gotta be real careful of them, though, Tessa, my girl.

These aren't your cheap discount-store dealies. They're the culmination of the shirtmaker's art. Primo quality!"

Tessa sifted flour so vigorously that clouds of white rose over the kitchen counter.

Casey put a couple of jars of cranberry juice on the counter. "Hey, take it easy, girlie! You're getting that flour all over everything."

Tessa slapped the flour sifter down on the counter. "I'm done," she said abruptly.

Casey clasped his hand to his stomach and exited suddenly without saying a word. We heard him slam the bathroom door. The plumbing gurgled.

"I've got to get out of here," said Stephen between clenched teeth, "or I'm going to say something I'll regret."

"Why don't you go for a walk," cried Tessa. "Penn, you'll go with him, won't you?"

"A walk? And have Casey coming along as soon as he gets out of the john? No, thanks," said Stephen. "I'm going to go out and do some target practice." He grinned. "I'll pretend Casey's head is the bull's-eye."

Casey was a long time in the bathroom. By the time he had returned, we could hear the pistol echoing in the woods.

"Something's wrong with my stomach," Casey grumbled.

Poison. The thought appeared in my mind full blown—if Casey drank poison, he would die and we wouldn't have to be afraid of him anymore. Color rushed to my face when I realized how pleasant the prospect was. I said quickly, "Why don't you lie down on the couch, Casey, and I'll fix you some tea."

Casey arranged himself on the sofa, an expression of settled discontent on his face. "Maybe I ate too fast. I got a couple of sausage biscuits, some ham and bacon, and a large coffee, and ate it on the way over."

"That's a big breakfast," said Tessa. "Why don't you take it easy for a while and give your stomach a chance to digest?"

"I guess I shouldn't have had the bacon," groaned Casey. "Does anybody around here have any antacid?"

It was the setup for countless mystery stories I had read—a character complains of indigestion and gulps something from a pill bottle. Instantly he becomes a corpse that smells like bitter almonds. It always turns out that the medicine was laced with cyanide.

I found a small bottle of antacid in the medicine cabinet in the bathroom. I was conscious of a mild regret that it smelled of mint and not of bitter almonds, but I was certainly not planning Casey's murder. Not then, anyway.

Penn put hot water on for tea, but before it came to the boil, snores rose from the sofa. Casey was fast asleep, his mouth open and his face flushed in pink blotches. He looked silly and helpless. Already I felt ashamed of my murderous fantasies.

Tessa dropped a damp dish towel over the bread dough she'd been kneading. "I think I'll go find Stephen," she said.

Penn and I went outside, too. The sun had burned the mist off the trees and river. A spray of wildflowers, mauve and white, lightened the shade just beyond the clearing. Tessa waved at us and disappeared in the direction of the pistol shots. On the other side of the clearing a small brown bird flicked its tail and poured out a liquid song.

"It's a Carolina wren," said Penn, glancing up. "Probably it's got a nest near here. They like to build close to the water."

It was getting hot, but we pressed past some bushes and stepped into the woods where it was cool and damp. "Stephen's quit shooting," said

Penn. "I guess Tessa's calmed him down."

"I wish Casey would lay off Stephen," I said.

"I wish he'd lay off me," said Penn. "I don't
dare let the things I've been buying Casey show
up on a charge-card bill, so I have to pack big
wads of cash. When I peel off the bills in
the store, you should see his eyes glitter.
Somehow he's got the idea I'm a bottomless pit
of money." We turned in the direction of the
river.

"What are you going to do?" I asked. The
restaurant meals alone, I realized, must be running into a lot of money. Hundreds of dollars.

"I don't know," said Penn.

"How can you keep this up?" I asked anxiously.

Penn made a helpless gesture. "I just don't
know." Leaves crackled noisily under our feet,
and small branches flew in our faces as we
pressed forward. A squirrel chattered at us, then
plunged noisily into some dry leaves. Its loud
voice sounded like a spiteful insult in the silence
of the woods.

After a while the river appeared through a
sunny opening in the woods ahead of us. We followed the curve of the land downward, and soon
we felt the water's coolness. Light filtered

through the trees in silver-dollar spots that threw unexpected bits of heat onto our heads and arms. Ferns sprouted in green, plushy carpets over a fallen tree. Its trunk had been split, and white wood thrust up to the sky like a splinter, a pointing finger where the shattered tree had stood. "Lightning," said Penn.

I scrambled over to the base of the tree and ran my hand over the clean white point of wood. The tree's trunk, fallen against the dirt, its bark loose and tattered, was unrecognizable. Already it was springing with a new life of soft green ferns.

"All the trees in the forest," said Penn, "and the lightning struck this one. Bad luck."

"Maybe the tree feels lucky," I said. "It's starting over."

"Yeah, as a rest home for ferns."

Ahead, the river was a band of light through the trees. Penn parted some branches and we were there, sunlight pouring onto the gleaming water. A bent tree leaned low over the flowing river, partly underwater. Its muddy branches showed how high the river had flooded weeks before.

I took off my shoes and began to pick my way down the slick bank, but I slipped and landed in

the black mud. Penn skidded down after me.
"Are you all right?" he asked.

"Yuck!" I made a face.

"Wash off in the river," suggested Penn. "But
be careful. Here, take hold of my hand."

The water was only up to my thighs at the
edge. Dry curled leaves floated lightly on the surface and spun in the eddies of water. "Turn
around," said Penn. "Your jeans are a mess."

I shrieked as he splashed cold water on the
back of my jeans. Then I wheeled and spanked
my hand on the water, splattering him. We
lunged at each other, splashing and laughing.
Penn took off his shirt and gave it to me, then
swam out to the tree and climbed up on it. His
bare flesh flashed white in the sunlight. His cut-
off jeans were dark and dripping.

"Come back!" I cried. The tree moved with
his weight as he dove in. In a moment his sleek
wet head surfaced, his hair slicked across his
eyes, and in long reaching strokes he swam back
to me. I felt his hand grab my leg under the surface. Then suddenly he stood up next to me,
streaming water.

The water dripping from his arm was pink,
and, startled, I gazed at a pulse of red blood
welling from his forearm. "You're hurt!" I cried.

Penn glanced down. "I must have caught it on the tree." He groped in his pocket and pulled out a handkerchief, but it was too wet to be much good sopping up the blood. I handed him his shirt, and he pressed it against the wound. The stain spread on the blue fabric of the shirt.

"Penn, it's still bleeding." My stomach squeezed painfully.

"Don't faint." He smiled. "It's only a scratch." He squeezed the wadded shirt material against his flesh, and his class ring winked in the uneven, leafy light. "We'd better get back to the cabin."

Our toes sank into the mud as we scrambled up the bank. We tried to wipe our wet feet first on leaves and then on our jeans, but it was a pretty hopeless business. My shoes felt squishy and grainy on the trek back. I went ahead, pushing branches out of the way because Penn was holding the wadded shirt against his bleeding arm.

He was telling me something about falling in the river when he was a kid, but I wasn't listening very closely. When he turned to check the trail, my eye traced the line of his nose and the delicate turn of his lip and chin. I wasn't used to

seeing Penn without his shirt. At the sight of his
muscular chest and flat stomach, I felt the color
rise on my cheeks. Yet under the warm love I felt
for Penn, I couldn't stop myself from thinking
how simple my life would be without him—no
police, no murder, no Casey. Only my father's
quiet house, where I would sit alone night after
night, the television and my diary my only company. I would go to school, take notes in class,
and eat alone in the cafeteria, while other people
around me had lives.

Penn stopped walking and turned to me. "Did
you ever do anything like that?" We were standing in deep shadow now and his eyes were shining in the darkness.

"Do what?" I asked, suddenly confused.

"You weren't listening!" he teased.

"I was looking at you," I confessed. I let a
branch slip out of my hands. It snapped toward
me with a sharp sound. The bloody shirt fell to
our feet as Penn put his arms around me. He
buried his face in my hair and blew puffs of air
through it until it tickled. "I like to look at you,
too," he said, chuckling. "What do you think
that means?"

"It must be love," I said.

When we kissed, my thoughts quit making

any sense. Lightning strikes, I thought, remembering the blasted tree. And afterward nothing is ever the same.

"We could come out here sometime, just the two of us," I said, uncertain as soon as I had spoken the words.

Slivers of light danced on the bare skin of his chest, and I could hear his breath coming fast. "Okay," he said. He folded me tightly into his arms and laughed unsteadily. "I love-you."

We didn't have far to go to the clearing, and only moments later we stepped out into the sunlight. The cabin lay directly ahead of us, bleached by the midday sun. I caught a glimpse of something red and looked down at my shirt in horror. Now, in the full light, I could see it was smeared with blood. The red was dotted in dark spots like exclamations and dragged thinly like a veil over the white shirt.

"You look like you've been shot," Penn said. "The cut must be deeper than I thought. I guess I'd better go into town and get it stitched."

Looking down at my bloody shirt, I felt so sick that I ran up the stairs, darted into my room, and tore it off. The blood had soaked through in places to the skin, leaving sticky pink spots on my skin.

The tape of Laurie's death began running in my mind. She was falling, grabbing at air. Her mouth opened wide but no scream came out. I shut my eyes tight and hugged myself.

Eleven

Dear Diary,

Am I making a terrible mistake? What if spending the night with Penn changes me forever?

Over at the sink of my bathroom vanity, my bloody shirt soaks in cold salty water. When I see the pink water, I remember the emergency room where Penn's arm got stitched up, and the bloody gauze there, lying in a stainless-steel bowl. The doctors and nurses all knew him. I suppose, when he was growing up, they had seen him at the hospital many times with his dad. It's hard to imagine, but once he was a stubby-legged toddler. Now he's a man and I love him. But if I am sure of *that, why am I so afraid of sleeping with him?*

On the fifteenth a thin letter was waiting for me when I got home from school. I ripped it open.

> Dear Joanna,
> Congratulations! You have been accepted as a member of Swarthmore's Class of 1999. This decision by the admissions committee reflects our confidence that you will make a valuable contribution to our community of learning.

I folded the letter and tucked it back in its envelope without reading the rest. I had already decided I didn't want to leave Penn to go far away to school.

My mind turned to Stephen, Tessa, and Casey. What were they finding in the mail today?

Penn drove up as I stood there. He leaned over the passenger seat and grinned at me through the open window. "Want a ride, lady?"

"Sure." I got in.

"Bad news for Stephen and Casey," he said as he turned the car around. I must have gone white, because he quickly added, "No, it's not the police. They haven't come around again yet. All I meant is Stephen got wait-listed at Princeton and Casey got turned down by MIT. Tessa got into Princeton, which is no surprise, with her dad being such a big-shot alumnus. Stephen's pretty bummed, but all things considered, I guess he's taking it okay. When I left him, he was plotting the bus schedules between Rutgers and Princeton. Casey's the one I'm worried about."

"You've seen him?"

"Not yet. I called over there and got his little sister. She's the one who told me about MIT. Casey wouldn't come to the phone. She said he's acting weird." He gave me a quick glance. "I figured maybe we'd better go over there."

Casey's family lived in an old two-story house. Out front a porch swing creaked on its rusty chains. A large maple cast a dark shadow over the front yard, and a climbing rose trailed a spindly, long green stem over the trellis behind the swing. A hanging basket of geraniums made a vivid splash of red in the shadows of the porch.

Penn banged on the door until it rattled. A girl of thirteen or so opened it. She was wearing sandals and a purple T-shirt that came down to her knees. Her hair was a tangled mess of copper curls, and the freckles sprinkled unevenly on her face were the same copper color. She surveyed us calmly. "Casey won't come out of his room," she said. "I called Mom at work, but she said to leave him alone." The music coming from upstairs was so loud, the ceiling was vibrating.

"Maybe he'll talk to us," said Penn.

We went upstairs, and Penn knocked on Casey's bedroom door. It was doubtful that Casey could hear anything over the loud music, so Penn pushed the door open and walked in. Casey sat on the floor, slumped against his bed. Books were all over the room, their pages splayed awkwardly. A poster taped to the wall had been ripped halfway down so that one half flapped loosely against the wall.

Penn turned the stereo down. "Are you all right, Casey?"

Casey gazed at us dully. A crust of dried blood glistened on his lip. "Sure. Go away," he said. His eyes were bloodshot, and the soft flesh around his eyes was pink and puffy.

Penn sat down on the bed while I stood awkwardly in the doorway, wishing I could leave.

"I know it's tough," Penn said. "But that's the way it goes. You don't kill yourself over what some stupid college says. Who cares? It's all a toss of the dice anyway. Get up and let's go get something to eat."

"If you're finished sounding like my mother, you can go," said Casey coldly.

"Look," said Penn, "it's a mistake to take it personally."

"Easy for you to say," said Casey thickly. "You get everything you go after. Girls. Cars. Grades. This is the only thing I ever wanted, and I didn't get it."

"You can get just as good an education at State—" began Penn.

But Casey cut him off, shrieking, "Get out of here! Get out of my room right this minute." Casey stood up and pawed at the top of his dresser, and I realized he was reaching for a brass bookend. Quickly I pulled Penn out of the room. A heavy thud struck against the door as we closed it.

"Phew!" said Penn.

Not knowing what else to do, we went downstairs. Casey's sister stood at the foot of the stairs and watched us descend. She sucked noisily on a lime Popsicle. "Mom said to leave him alone," she said.

"Right," said Penn. "Well, maybe we had better stay away from him for a while, Chrissy. He's pretty upset."

"Mom says Casey always goes overboard," said Chrissy.

I was glad to close the door to the big dark house with its high thin Victorian windows that reminded me uncomfortably of my mother's house. "I can't believe the way he's taking it," I said when we were outside, breathing fresh air. "There are other schools. It's not a question of life and death."

"Yeah, but Casey's been planning on MIT since he was in elementary school." Penn glanced up at the broad-branching maple.

"I could understand him being upset," I said. "But he's practically psychotic!"

"I've got to admit I'm worried," said Penn slowly.

On the other side of the street a black cat picked its way through a bed of daffodils.

The next morning I was walking to class when I noticed Bobby in front of my locker talking to Koo. His shaggy head was bent over her as if he were listening intently. What could they be talking about? I wanted to know, but I was afraid to get close enough to find out.

A loud metallic bang sounded suddenly, and I jumped. Koo went on talking to Bobby as if she hadn't heard it—she was not easily rattled—but then I noticed uneasily that the door of my locker was badly bent. Bobby had kicked it!

The destruction of my locker didn't cause a ripple in the flow of traffic in the hallway. No one stopped to check it out. Maybe they were afraid to look at Bobby, afraid he'd hit them. I backed away and bumped into somebody. "Excuse me," I muttered, flustered.

I decided that Bobby and Koo must be talking about Laurie. Somehow I didn't want to know what they were saying anymore. All I wanted was to get away from them as fast as possible. Bobby's explosive outburst had made a chill of fear creep up my spine. I walked away quickly, pressing my way past clumps of people in the busy hallway. I wished I could forget the enraged look on Bobby's face.

That afternoon the group met at The Bakery—except for Casey. The low afternoon light streamed in the windows onto the brick walls and the rough wooden tables. It was a quiet scene that seemed a million miles away from the violent one I had witnessed by my locker that morning. I couldn't stop thinking about Bobby. If he had the slightest suspicion Penn was mixed up in Laurie's death . . . The thought had me panicked.

"This is perfect," said Tessa, her mouth full. "Don't you love the smell of fresh-baked bread? Jasmine tea and lumps of sugar. Mmm. Utter heaven."

"Believe me," said Stephen, "today is a day I need comfort food." He buttered a piece of bread and stuffed it in his mouth. He had been smoking so heavily, he smelled as if he had been pulled from a burning building. "Did I mention the police yanked me out of class this afternoon?" he asked.

Penn and I stared at him. "I thought they had given up!" I cried. "What did they say?"

"It was pretty bad." Stephen took a deep breath. "They took me to the police station, and I had to wait a long time in a little room with just a plain table and a chair. Finally this guy named Lewis came in. I used to think he was the nice one—he always calls me son. He asked if I realized that conspiracy and withholding of evidence are crimes."

"What did you say?" I cried.

"I was so staggered, I didn't know what to say. I had this sinking feeling Casey had squealed."

There was a painful silence.

"What happened?" asked Penn finally.

"Well, it hit me that if Casey had squealed, I was going to be arrested anyway, so it wasn't as if keeping my mouth shut could make anything worse. So I said I didn't know what he was talking about, but that he was scaring me to death. I said maybe I should ask my parents to call a lawyer." I noticed that Stephen's hands were shaking. Evidently he did, too, because he hastily put down his cup. "Then this Officer Lewis got very earnest and confidential—the 'sons' flew fast and furious—and told me it was best to come clean, because it would go easier with me when the truth came out if I had cooperated with the police, and if there was anything I wanted to say to him, I should say it now and he would do the best he could to help me out."

Penn stared at him. "They didn't say anything like that to me."

"Maybe they're afraid of your father," said Tessa. "He has plenty of clout in this town."

"Maybe," said Stephen bitterly. "But it could

be that they're hitting at the weakest link. I don't pretend I come across all cool like Penn. I probably look like I'd spill everything with a little prodding. Luckily, despite appearances to the contrary, I managed to keep from breaking down and confessing. But I had to sit there for what seemed like hours trying to convince this Officer Lewis that I'm just an innocent kid who doesn't have a clue what he's getting at. All the time I was sweating like a pig."

"Jeez," said Penn softly, "if they try that line with Casey, we're dead. He's already in pretty bad shape."

"Where *is* Casey?" said Tessa. "I haven't seen him for days."

"He's spending a lot of time in the computer lab," said Penn.

"Penn went looking for him last night and found him there," I explained. "He said he was working on some programs for the school."

"But he said it with a smirk," added Penn.

"Th-that's all we need," said Stephen. "Casey gets caught hacking. The cops will be crazy about that."

I glanced at Penn in alarm. "Do you think that's what he's doing, Penn? Hacking?"

"Probably," he admitted.

"Maybe he really is working on some programs for the school, like he says," I suggested. "It's possible, isn't it?" My hopeful remark was greeted with disbelief.

"Please, don't let him try to break into NASA's computers," Tessa said. "If the Feds come down on us, I truly do not think I can handle it."

"So, is Casey going with us for another jolly weekend at the cabin?" asked Stephen. "Or are you to have the pleasure of entertaining him at yet another pretentious restaurant?"

Penn cleared his throat. "I thought we'd skip the cabin this weekend," he said.

"Oh?" Tessa raised her brows.

"Joanna and I have plans," said Penn.

I could feel myself getting hot all over, which somewhat undercut Penn's dignified words.

Tessa's and Stephen's eyes dropped and at once they began feverishly buttering their bread. I'm sure they didn't realize how funny their obvious tactfulness was.

After a moment Penn said, "I hope the police don't suddenly decide to give me the third degree this weekend."

Tessa gave me a quick glance. "See? Even Penn is nervous. Anybody would be nervous with the police hounding us. I keep telling

Stephen, nervousness is entirely normal—the police know that."

"I should go talk to them now, then," said Stephen feelingly. "If they like nervous, they'd love me. I'm so freaking nervous, if you breathed on me I'd fall apart."

Friday morning I was startled to run into Casey at my locker. "Casey!" I cried. "Where've you been? I haven't seen you in days. Have you given up eating lunch or something?"

He shrugged. "I've just been grabbing a sandwich and eating at the computer. So, where's Koo?" He looked around. "Doesn't she come by here before class?"

I got my books out of the locker and straightened up, vaguely conscious something was different. Usually when I stood up there, my nose was filled with the distinctive odors that radiated from the paper bags Koo kept stashed at the bottom of the locker. Today, I got a beery whiff instead. Then I got a look at Casey's glazed eyes and it hit me. Casey had been drinking.

The last time I had seen Casey drink was at one of Bobby's parties. He was stumbling drunk and riding Koo around on his shoulders. Worse, he had babbled about his illegal hacking exploits. It was not a comforting memory.

I spotted Koo coming in our direction. She was wearing a clingy black print gabardine sundress, but she had unbuttoned the bottom eight or so buttons of it so her white legs flicked out through the open dress as she strode in our direction.

"Hi, there, Casey," she drawled.

Casey turned to me. "Get lost, will you, Jo-Jo? Koo and I want to be alone."

As I waited for Penn in the cafeteria, I scribbled a quick entry in my diary.

> . . . I'm so nervous about spending the weekend with Penn at the cabin, I can hardly think of anything else, but the whiff of alcohol I got off Casey is making alarm bells go off in my brain. I've never heard of anybody drinking so early in the morning. What's happening? And why is Casey getting back together with Koo?

I put my pen down as I saw Penn entering the lunchroom. "Casey was waiting for Koo at the locker this morning," I told him, "and he'd been drinking."

"Liquor and Koo," said Penn. "Two bad ideas

at once." He pulled me close to him and landed a careless kiss on my ear.

"Woo-woo-woo," said a freckle-eared boy, pushing past us.

Penn's eyes crinkled into amused triangles. "Whenever I think about us going out to the cabin together, not even Casey can bring me down," he said.

I smiled at him and looked quickly away. Going to the cabin with Penn had seemed like a wonderful idea back when I suggested it, on that walk in the woods. I had felt so overcome with love for him. But now I was getting a bad case of cold feet. All the sex-education films I had ever seen were fast-forwarding in my brain—films on AIDS, teen pregnancy, date rape. I also remembered all the improbable diagrams of the male and female anatomy I had been shown since seventh grade. What was I getting myself into?

I must be very odd, I decided. Didn't I trust Penn? Didn't I love him? In spite of myself, I looked around me at kids stuffing food in their mouths. Maybe it was because I was worried about having sex that I was suddenly focusing on the human body at its most basic—cramming food in its mouth. I had never thought before how ugly teeth and lips were, or how disgusting it was to see bits of chewed food as people talked.

When she sat down, I scarcely saw Tessa across the table. Instead, as if a film were running behind my eyes, I saw Laurie falling very slowly, as if she were sinking in a poisonous liquid. I could see her face, with its wild eyes and open mouth. Long blond hair was floating over her head, and her cheekbones showed under her thin fair skin, fine and angled upward, like wings. Laurie had my face!

"Are you okay?" Tessa asked me.

Her voice banished the troubling images. What was going on? I wondered. Was the idea of sleeping with Penn making me feel unsafe? As if I were about to lose control and fall off a cliff? Or did some secret part of my brain wonder if Penn had told me the whole truth about Laurie's death? My head was spinning, and it took a minute for me to focus on what the others were saying.

"Joanna tells me Casey had liquor on his breath this morning," said Penn, "and it looks like he's getting back up with Koo."

"That's pretty bad," said Tessa uneasily.

Stephen leaned over the table. "I don't

know about you, but I'm not about to sit around and let Casey send me to prison for twenty years," he said. "Has it occurred to you that we'd better have some kind of plan for dealing with him?"

"He's still in shock over that MIT thing." Penn looked uncomfortable. "He'll get over it. Remember the last time he started hanging out with Koo? We panicked, but nothing happened. They broke up in days."

"We may not be so lucky this time," fretted Tessa.

"Look!" hissed Tessa. "There they are!" We all followed her horrified gaze. Five or six tables closer to the front of the cafeteria, Koo was whispering in Casey's ear. Suddenly Casey climbed up on his chair and stepped onto the cafeteria table. Abruptly he bent over, and a second later I saw a sock and a shoe fly into the air.

"Yuck," said Tessa, her attention riveted. "His smelly feet on the table! That is disgusting."

A bunch of kids had gathered around the table Casey was standing on. They seemed to be chanting something softly in unison. A steady low noise was discernible from the excited babble of the cafeteria. In a single motion Casey pulled his black turtleneck over his head. He stood there a moment with his arms lifted overhead, immobilized by the knit shirt, and then gave a jerk of his skinny hips and shimmied. Someone whooped.

"He's cracked," said Stephen flatly

Casey let the shirt drop to the table. His audience was chanting louder now, and I could hear what they were saying: "Take it off." The cafeteria staff had come out and were standing against the wall with their arms folded, gazing in amazement at Casey's bony white chest.

"More, more, more!" cried the kids around his table.

Casey's belt fell to the table, and then his pants dropped around his ankles, revealing that his underwear of choice was candy-striped boxer shorts. The cafeteria was hushed momentarily. Kids held their breath, not wanting to miss a moment of a stunt that was clearly destined to become a school legend. Suddenly Casey cringed and a fiery blush colored his neck and shoulders. He stooped hastily and pulled his pants up. Giggling, Koo handed him his shoes and shirt. I lost sight of them in the crowd for a minute, but then I saw them again. Casey, still bare-chested, pushed the cafeteria side door open, and they ducked out.

Stephen's mouth was twitching. "I know it's not funny," he said unsteadily. "But I can't help it. It's classic!"

"He's bound to get suspended," I said. "Not only is doing a striptease in the cafeteria a heinous violation of every school rule in the book—"

Tessa giggled suddenly. "'Appropriate attire must be worn'—chapter one of the school handbook."

"Okay, it's funny." Penn's voice was flat. "But it's got to mean he's totally cracking up. What are we going to do?"

. . . Casey is cracking up! Penn's words made me even more scared than I already was. Casey was dangerous before, but now he's like a time bomb. And we're all so helpless. What can any of us do? Maybe Penn could persuade him to go to an AA meeting. Or Tessa could talk to him. But even as I write down these commonsense solutions, I know it's no use. It's as if he were some great natural force, like a tidal wave. I can't honestly imagine that anything we do will make any difference.

I guess I'm in no shape to come up with

a solution to the Casey problem right now. I'm worrying so much about my weekend with Penn that my problem-solving skills aren't in full gear. It's probably the same with Penn, right? He must be thinking non-stop about being with me.

Twelve

Dear Diary,

The weekend with Penn is going to be fine. Besides, it's too late for me to back out. I would look so stupid! I wish I could recapture the warm and loving feeling I had when I first suggested it—but that happy afternoon in the woods seems like a lifetime ago.

I keep thinking about Laurie. Penn was right there when she died! Couldn't he have somehow stopped her from falling? How can I be sure he's telling me the truth?

Saturday morning, while my father was still asleep, the phone rang. I grabbed it.

"Joanna? This is Penn." I knew from the sound of his voice that something was wrong.

"I'm afraid I won't be there on time to pick you up," he said. "The police want me to go downtown with them to answer a few questions. I'm not sure how long it will take."

"Are they there now?" I asked. "Can you talk?"

"Yes, that's right," he said. "I'll get away as soon as I can."

After I hung up, I sat for a moment in the kitchen listening to my heartbeat. Then I called Tessa's number. A child answered the phone. Saturday-morning cartoons sounded shrill in the background. "Tessie!" screamed the childish voice.

There was a click, and the cartoon sounds abruptly stopped. "Hello?" Tessa said.

"Tessa, it's Joanna. The police have got Penn."

"W-what exactly do you mean by that?" she stuttered.

"They've taken him downtown for questioning!"

"Oh." She sounded relieved. "They did that with Stephen, too, remember? He told us all about it."

I suddenly remembered Penn's notion that our phones might be tapped. I looked up at the globe light fixture that hung over the kitchen table and saw reflected on its blank white surface a tiny, pale image of the trees and the pond outside the window, as if the world outside had shrunk and lost its color. I felt myself choke up. "I guess I just needed somebody to talk to," I said.

"Do you want me to come over?" offered Tessa with quick sympathy.

"That would be nice," I gulped.

Tessa and I sat in my living room. I didn't want to leave the house in case Penn should call.

My father appeared in a knit shirt, beige slacks, and golf shoes. He raised his eyebrows when he saw Tessa. "Hullo," he said vaguely. "I'm going to be lunching at the club."

"We may not be here when you get back," I said, not looking up. "We're talking about going to the cabin for the weekend." A lump rose in my throat. What if we weren't going to the cabin ever again? What if they had arrested Penn?

"So you and Penn are going out to the cabin?" Tessa asked when my father had left.

"I don't know. What does it matter?" I asked desperately. "He's been at the station for hours.

It's almost lunchtime. What can they have been doing all this time?"

The doorbell rang, and I leapt up.

"Sorry, it's only me," said Stephen when I flung the door open. "Any word yet?"

I shook my head.

"Damn," said Stephen.

I blinked and looked away, overcome suddenly by a vision of Penn writhing under hot lights.

"You look terrible, Joanna. Hang in there. We're going to get through this okay." Stephen kissed my cheek.

"He's been at the station for hours," said Tessa. "What can be taking so long?"

"Maybe they're having a fire drill. Do you have anything to eat around here?" asked Stephen.

"Eggs, I guess," I said. "And there's bacon in the freezer."

Soon the smell of bacon cooking drifted through the open kitchen door into the living room. Stephen came out of the kitchen with a plate of scrambled eggs and bacon. He perched on one of the modern chairs. Tessa was on her knees by the coffee table, concentrating on a magazine. I stared out the window, hoping to see

Penn's Corvette. After a while Stephen got up, and I heard a clatter of dishes and running water. He came back and sat down. "Do you care if I smoke?"

"Maybe we'd better go out on the deck," I said.

I flung the kitchen windows open so I could be sure of hearing the phone and the doorbell.

The sky was a startling contrast of black and white, with the sun shining next to a bank of threatening clouds. The surface of the pond shimmered. A sudden splash sounded and the dark dot of a turtle's head surfaced in the water. A small V-shape wake pointed to where it was swimming.

Stephen leaned against the deck railing, struck a match, and lit his cigarette. Soon his head was enveloped in a blue-gray haze.

"Don't you ever try to quit?" I asked him.

He smiled and blew out the match. "Constantly."

"My prayers have not been answered," said Tessa ironically.

"I guess Tessa will go off and find herself some short-haired Ivy Leaguer who plays volleyball and lives the clean life." Stephen's cigarette clung to his bottom lip as he spoke.

"Don't start, Stephen," said Tessa tightly.

"Tessa thinks I'm getting paranoid. Maybe I am." Stephen flicked his cigarette away. "Don't you wonder if we're making a mistake, letting Casey go off by himself? I didn't like it much that he was pigging out at expensive restaurants every night and soaking Penn for fancy shirts, but this is worse. We don't have a clue what he's doing. What if he's already gone to the cops?"

"Don't say that!" My throat tightened.

"I saw Casey last night," said Tessa.

Stephen stared. "You didn't tell me that."

"When I got the shirts ironed, I took them over to the computer lab," Tessa said. "I didn't mention it, because I knew it would make you mad."

Stephen sucked greedily on the cigarette. "He's got a nerve, giving you his dirty laundry."

Tessa unfolded an aluminum chair and sat down facing us, shielding her eyes from the sun with her hand. "My mother thought it was pretty strange. I had to slave over a hot iron the better part of the week to get all those shirts done, so it wasn't as if I could hide it. She asked why I was ironing Casey's shirts."

"What story did you give her?" Stephen drew deeply on his cigarette, his eyes narrowing.

"I said I had offered to do it to cheer him up," said Tessa. "Because he was so down about being rejected by MIT. But I think she's decided I have a secret passion for Casey."

"Great!" said Stephen. "That's all I need." He tossed the cigarette away.

"Naturally, she's concerned about my sanity," Tessa joked.

"How did Casey seem?" I interrupted her. "Did he mention Laurie at all?"

"No, he was full of himself about the striptease in the cafeteria," said Tessa. "He's famous now, and he thinks that's cool."

Stephen struck a match, and as it flamed out he cupped a hand over it and lit another cigarette. He drew on it and exhaled smoke through his nose. "I'm surprised they haven't thrown him out of school," he said. "Did he explain how he managed to keep from getting suspended?"

"He threw himself on Mr. Hansen's mercy and claimed he was suffering from severe emotional distress," said Tessa. "That must have been easy. It's the truth. He probably looked completely deranged in the principal's office. But he played it to me as a cunning move. He was smirking with every syllable." She paused thoughtfully. "They're completely dependent on him for all the fancy computer work, which may have had something to do with their letting him off, don't you think?"

"Could you tell whether he had talked to the police?" I asked. The water splashed as a panicked frog bolted from the pond.

"I don't think he had," said Tessa. "Unless he's playing a very deep game."

Just then I heard the electric *dong* of the doorbell. I ran to the front door. When I flung it open, Penn stepped inside. "What are Stephen and Tessa doing over here?" he asked abruptly.

"They're keeping me company. We were all so worried." My eyes searched his face. "Are you okay? What did the police say?"

"It was a nightmare," he said.

Tessa and Stephen came in the back door and stood beside it, silhouetted against the window.

"Well, they didn't arrest me. That's the bright side." A muscle at the corner of his eye twitched. "They left me in a little room for about an hour. All the time, I'm thinking they've come up with something really bad— new evidence or something—and I'm totally freaking out. So then I get a glimmer of hope. I think maybe it's only that the cops changed shifts. Maybe they don't remember I'm in here.

Finally I go out to the front desk and ask what was going on." He frowned. "Have you got any coffee or anything, Joanna?"

I shot Tessa a look. Penn never drank coffee. In the kitchen cabinet I found a small jar of instant that had gone mostly hard, but I was able to chip off about a teaspoonful and melt it in a mug of hot water. Little brown foamy bits floated on top. Penn took it, and sat on the edge of a leather chair. "A woman in uniform at the desk said they were busy and they'd be with me before long," he said. "So I went back to the room and waited another half hour. I got a cup of coffee out of a machine, but there wasn't even anything to read in there. Finally two policemen came in and sat down across from me." Penn cradled the mug in both hands and awkwardly took a sip, wiping the little bits of dried coffee off his mouth with the back of his hand. "One of them was short and fat and sweating hard. He leaned toward me the whole time with his hands braced on his knees. He seemed like the fatherly type. The other one was younger with short blond hair.

"Just when I think I've decided which is the good guy and which is the bad guy, the fatherly one started telling me I'd better not think I'm getting away with anything, because murderers always get caught."

Stephen fell back against his chair abruptly, as if he had been slapped. "Isn't there a law against this kind of thing? Don't they have to warn you of your rights or something?"

Penn gave a short humorless laugh. "Funny, the same thing occurred to me. I kept telling myself if this were really serious, they would warn me of my rights. But—I don't know—I guess I couldn't convince myself that it was going to be okay. I was a wreck—my palms were even sweaty."

"I wonder why they haven't called me in." Tessa shivered. "Maybe I'm next. I don't think I'm going to be good at this."

"Come off it, Tess," said Stephen. "You're tough as nails. So what was the line of questioning? Could you tell what they were getting at?"

"They didn't exactly lay any clues at my feet, if that's what you mean. The blond guy started talking softly, and said that they understood how people didn't like to tell on their friends, but that I would never go wrong by being honest with the police. Then he started saying how proud my mom and dad were of me and how he was sure I wouldn't want to let them down. I thought I was going to burst into tears."

"But you aren't even that close to your parents!" protested Tessa.

"Maybe that was what got to me," said Penn.

"Jeez!" said Stephen.

"They took out our old statements and showed me this list of discrepancies." He put the mug down on the fireplace hearth.

"What discrepancies?" whispered Tessa, sinking onto the couch.

"Little things," Penn shrugged. "Nothing important. I said it was hard to remember exactly what happened on what seemed like a perfectly ordinary day at the time, and that I wasn't surprised our accounts didn't always jibe."

"They should jibe," insisted Tessa. "We went over it and over it."

"Yes." Penn smiled. "If you ask me, the really suspicious thing was that we all pretty much gave the same story. It's not natural for the witnesses to give the same story. I think usually they contradict each other all over the place." His smile disappeared. "Then they asked me about the letter Laurie's mom got. I did okay with that; I expect I sounded pretty upset. I said it was cruel."

"Did they mention Casey at all?" I asked.

"I don't think they've gotten around to him yet. Maybe they really are busy, the way the woman at the desk claimed."

"If they had solid evidence," I said, "they wouldn't be bringing you into the police station one by one and trying to get you to confess. They must be desperate."

"Maybe," said Penn. "They could be pulling the same stunt with everybody, just hoping that one of us cracks."

"When they get to Casey," said Stephen bleakly, "they may get their wish."

Penn shrugged. "I can't worry about that now," he said.

"Nice for you," said Stephen sarcastically. "I can't stop worrying about it."

"Maybe what we need is a cup of tea," Tessa said.

"You can drink a gallon of tea if you want," said Penn. "But Joanna and I are out of here."

I had forgotten all about our planned weekend at the cabin, and I had to go back to my room to get my overnight bag. When I returned to the living room, Tessa and Stephen were leaving. Tessa gave us a sweet smile and a quick wave.

*   *   *

. . . It's a small thing, but I can't remember Penn ever telling the others to make themselves scarce before. His rudeness when he said "Drink a gallon of tea if you want" probably shows how strung out he is. But I feel something has changed. The attitude of "all for one and one for all" that made our group so tight knit has shifted slightly and been replaced by something not quite sturdy.

Penn was silent as we drove out of town. Beads of sweat glistened on his face, and he stared ahead so steadily at the road that I wasn't sure he even remembered that I was in the car. At last he spoke. "I'm afraid I didn't do too well with the police."

My heart stopped. "Did they *say* anything to you?"

"Not exactly," he said. "It was more the way the blond one looked at me when I was getting up to leave."

"He was trying to scare you, that's all."

"No, it wasn't that. They had finished with me. It was just chance that I caught a glimpse of him out of the corner of my eye. He had a funny expression—as if he were doing a math problem in his head. He was trying that hard to figure me out. I guess he was thinking that something about me didn't quite add up. Or maybe he just didn't like the smell of me." He paused for a second and checked the rearview mirror. "I could almost see his lip curl—you know, as if he had already decided I was scum. The man didn't like me."

"But I thought the blond was the nice one!" I cried.

"That was only an act," said Penn impatiently. "Good guy–bad guy. Haven't you seen them do that in movies?"

"I don't see why he wouldn't like you," I protested. "I like you."

Penn squeezed my knee. "Yeah, but I don't think he finds me quite as attractive as you do." He frowned suddenly. "The thing is, Tessa may be right. Maybe it does look better to those guys if you're nervous. It could be they thought I was a little too cool."

"But you were nervous!"

"I know. But I'll bet it didn't show."

I knew what he meant. When Penn got really upset, it was as if a shutter closed down to hide his feelings. He had a way of looking cool even when he was falling apart inside.

He glanced at me. "The guy was probably

tagging me as an emotionless psychopathic serial killer."

"No! He couldn't think that!" I took a deep breath. "Besides, it doesn't matter whether they like you or not. They have to have evidence before they bring any charges, right?"

"I hope," said Penn. "But it's clear we're all being watched." He took a deep breath. "If anything goes wrong—"

"Don't think about that!" I said quickly. "Nothing is going to go wrong."

Neither of us spoke Casey's name, but we didn't have to. We both knew all too well what might go wrong.

Thirteen

*. . . Funny. For days I've been asking myself
if I'm making a big mistake to come out to
the cabin with Penn. But now I know I'm
not. Penn needs me. And I need him.*

Penn stood at the big window that looked out
on the river. The silence was awful. I sat by the
cold fireplace, leafing through an old news-
magazine someone had left weeks before.
Outside, a dove made a shrill rattling sound as it
rose in flight.

"I guess I'm not very good company today."
Penn turned to face me. "Should I make some
lunch?"

"It doesn't matter." I closed the magazine.
"Penn, isn't there some way you could leave the

country if this all blows up in our faces?"

"Would you come with me?" He smiled faintly.

"Sure." My heart sank at the thought. Hurried attempts to get a passport. Confused and lost in a strange country. Afraid of every policeman. "How would we do it?" I was suddenly having trouble catching my breath. "Where could we go?"

"Nowhere." He shook his head ruefully. "I've thought it all out, and there isn't any way to get out of the country. We can't get work permits; and even if I took every dime I had out of the bank, it wouldn't keep us forever. Besides, I bet I couldn't take that kind of money out without somebody at the bank picking up the phone and calling my father."

"I thought banking transactions were supposed to be confidential."

"Dream on. Nothing is confidential in a town like this." The strained look around his eyes gave me a pang.

I shifted my position in the chair. "There's got to be something we can do."

"Get rid of Casey."

I stared at him, taken aback.

*   *   *

. . . Maybe Penn isn't who I think he is.
How can I know him so well and suddenly
be hit by the feeling that I don't know him
at all?

"You don't have to look at me like that."
Penn ran his fingers through his hair restlessly.
"I'm not planning to murder Casey. But you can
see how the thought might pop into my mind
now and then."

I recalled my faint disappointment that the
antacid I had given Casey was not poison. "I've
had a thought or two myself in that direction," I
admitted.

"All that stuff with the computers was his
idea, and now that it's all gone bad, he's turned
on us," said Penn bitterly. "I'm as much his pris-
oner as his keeper. I keep thinking maybe I
shouldn't have come out here this weekend because I should be keeping an eye on Casey."

I had crossed my ankle over my knee, and I
noticed, as if my legs belonged to someone else,
that my foot was jerking. Abruptly I sat up
straight and planted both feet firmly on the floor.
"Nothing will keep him happy, Penn," I said.
"Not since he got turned down by MIT."

Penn gave a short laugh and paced a few

steps back and forth in front of the window. The river ran dark under an overcast sky. Penn glanced swiftly at me. "That striptease in the cafeteria—could you believe it? And he's gotten away with it. He seems to get away with everything."

Penn was right, I realized. Casey did get away with everything—no wonder he was so full of himself. He probably figured he could turn in Penn and the others and walk away whistling a tune.

I thought a moment and then spoke hesitantly. "It's not just that, Penn. He's acting as if nothing matters anymore. Like those people during the Black Plague who got drunk and caroused."

"Not a very comforting thought," said Penn.

"Do you want to drive back to town right now? If it's bothering you, we could check on him."

"I don't want to do that." He looked at me seriously. "Do you?"

I shook my head.

Penn laughed. "Then come here."

I got up and went over to him. He put his hands on my shoulders and kissed me fiercely, which surprised me. It was so unlike him, but I found myself kissing him back with the same force. His hand was behind my neck, pressing me hard against him. He tasted bitter, of black coffee. With his other hand, he groped to unbutton my shirt, and I felt my heart quickening. From that instant I forgot about Casey, forgot about everything except Penn and me.

Afterward I got embarrassed and pulled the sheet up to my chin. It was too bad, I thought, that I was so skinny I could count all my ribs. But Penn pulled the sheet away, and began counting "This little piggy went to market" on my toes. It tickled, and I squirmed away, accidentally rocking the nightstand. The box of condoms fell to the floor, and we both laughed.

The bedroom curtain billowed suddenly, as if it were haunted by the wind, and my laughter died. A cold thought visited me as suddenly as the breeze, and I knew I was going to voice it, even though I knew I was making a mistake. "Penn?"

He looked at me through sleepy eyes, a smile twitching at his lips. "Uh-huh?"

"Have you done this before?"

His face froze. Abruptly he reached for his

bathrobe, swung his feet around off the bed, and shrugged the robe on. His hair was in damp, dark points at the nape of his neck.

"Well," I said. "Have you?"

"Yes," he said.

"Who with?" It was as if some evil genie were inside me, making me say these things when I didn't want to hear the answers. I hated myself for asking. I was thinking of how Tessa had teased Penn about having a fling with Koo. I couldn't stop thinking about them together in this bed.

Penn tied the robe closed, then turned around to face me, one leg crooked on the bed. His face suddenly softened. "You don't want to hear about it."

"Yes. Yes, I do."

"No, you don't. And it doesn't matter. This is completely different, because we're in love. Right?"

"You weren't in love with the other girls?"

Penn snorted. "Come on, Joanna, stop it."

"Was it Koo?"

"Joanna! Give me a break, okay? I'm not asking you questions about your mother, am I?"

I clutched the crumpled sheet to my chest. A hot tear spilled onto my cheek. "I don't know what's the matter with me," I choked.

He put his arm around me and pulled me close. His breath ruffled my hair. "Nothing's the matter with you. You're absolutely terrific and I love you."

"I'm stupid."

Penn laughed. "Okay, you're stupid. We're both stupid. Did you eat any lunch?"

I lifted my tear-streaked face and met his eyes. "How could I eat when you were getting the third degree at the police station?"

"Probably your blood sugar is low. That's what's making you morbid. Let's go get some food."

Penn and I went into the kitchen and began opening and closing cabinets. "Cookies, pretzels, cheese. That's pretty much what's on hand. And I got some stuff from the deli, too. What sounds good?"

We went out to the car together, the wood steps feeling warm under my bare feet. The sky was heavily overcast, which drained the spring color from the trees and made them dark. A fresh breeze blew the skirt of my bathrobe, exposing the bare flesh of my thigh. I cast a self-conscious look toward the road, but the road was empty. Bits of pebble in the driveway bit into my feet. "I'd better go in and put some clothes on," I said.

Penn's eyes crinkled with laughter. "No! I like you this way."

I grabbed a bag of groceries and scurried up the stairs. Wind moved in the trees, rising and falling, with a sound like a silk skirt brushing along the floor. As I groped for the door handle, suddenly a thud made me turn around sharply.

"A bird hit the window," said Penn, glancing up at it.

I looked down the steps. A small bird was huddled on the leaves piled up against the base of the house. The bird's feathers were fluffed up, its eye was bright, and I could see the soft movement of its chest—it was still breathing. A few feathers were stuck to the window where it had hit.

"It just needs to rest," said Penn, coming up the steps behind me. "It's in shock. I want to get hold of some of those stickers that are in the shape of hawks. That's supposed to warn them away from plate glass. I hate it when they break their necks."

I was glad the tiny bird had not broken its neck. My own sense of well-being felt fragile and birdlike. When I went inside, a sharp gust swept in behind me and ruffled the pages of the magazine.

Penn laid a round plastic tray on the counter and peeled off the clear plastic wrap, and I ducked back into the bedroom to retrieve my clothes. I hadn't been in Penn's room before, and I was surprised at its elegant touches, the white eyelet curtains at the window and the white crocheted bedspread laid over blue sheets. I realized that this bedroom, with the queen-sized bed, must have belonged to his parents. The other two bedrooms had simple, rustic furniture. I was startled to catch movement out of the corner of my eye, but when I wheeled around, it was only my own image caught in the mirror of a dressing table—a fair girl with serious eyes. A pitcher sat in a shallow bowl on the dressing table, and a set of combs and brushes. Self-conscious, now that I could see myself in the mirror, I stooped to pick my clothes off the floor. Some underwear was still missing, so I got down on my knees and fished under the bed for it. I pulled out my missing bra, but along with it came a puff of dust and a pair of scanty black-lace panties. I sat there, frozen, on the floor, staring at them and feeling my pulse beat in my throat.

"Come eat!" called Penn.

I glanced toward the open door. An unutterable weariness had settled on me like paralysis, and I was sure I couldn't move. I heard Penn's voice. Then he stepped to the door, his brows creased in puzzlement. "Joanna? Aren't you—" His voice halted suddenly when he saw me. Tears prickled my eyes.

"What's wrong?" he cried, but then he followed my gaze to the black-lace panties, which were spread on the floor like an ad for lingerie. He scooped them up off the floor and held them in one hand, bewildered.

"You don't recognize them?" I whispered.

"I swear—honestly, Joanna, this is strange." He pushed his hair out of his eyes distractedly with his forearm. He looked so harassed that suddenly I actually believed him.

I struggled to my feet.

As if he had forgotten me, Penn stared out the window with a faraway look. The curtains flapped sharply in the breeze. "It's Casey," he said flatly. "He's brought some girl out here."

"How could he do that?" I cried. "He doesn't have a key, does he?"

"He must have made a copy of the key somehow. That's got to be what happened." Penn turned to me. "Joanna, I swear to you—"

"It's okay. I believe you." I hugged my clothes to my chest and fled to the bathroom.

Somehow I didn't want to dress in front of him. I needed to be alone to have a chance to collect myself. I threw the bathroom window open and let the fresh air blow in. The large mirror over the bathroom vanity was mottled at the bottom, damaged by the moisture of too many steamy showers. The vanity, like the flooring, was bare wood, a white sink with cabinets below.

I climbed into my jeans and snapped them. I sneezed suddenly and saw a faint haze rise in the air, so faint I blinked quickly, wondering if I had imagined it. It was then I realized that a thin film of white lay over the wood of the vanity. I ran my hand over its surface. When I lifted my palm, ovals of white stretched along my fingers and a circle of white dotted the heel of my hand.

"Penn!" I called.

I heard his running footsteps, and the door flew open. I held up my hand for him to see.

"Jeez, what next?" He paled. "Cocaine?"

I stretched out my tongue and touched it to my palm.

"No!" cried Penn. "Don't taste it!"

"It's rice powder, I think."

"Is that something you cook with?" he asked, confused. "Cooking, you mean like Tessa?" He shook his head. "No, it doesn't make sense. I can't believe Tessa would wear black-lace underwear, can you? She's not the black-lace-underwear type."

As it happened, I knew that Tessa's tastes ran to see-through bits of sheer nylon. "Rice powder is a kind of Japanese face powder," I said. "You use it to get a dead white look."

"Koo." Penn flushed. "I knew it had to be Casey. He's brought Koo out here—I'll kill him."

The cottage had no phone, so Penn and I drove to the nearest service station, some ten miles away, and from there called a locksmith. Penn was silent and white with rage. We drove back to the cottage then to wait in silence for the locksmith.

Penn opened the fridge. I heard the loud clatter of ice cubes and then a soft fizzing as he poured a drink over the ice. "Casey wants to take everything I have," Penn said. "He's trying to bleed me of every cent, and then he comes out here and— If he can't take it away from me, he wants to ruin it for me."

The locksmith's van drove up and Penn went outside to meet him. The locksmith was a short man with a large nose and a face worn by time. He looked so much like a gnome, he might have stepped out of a tree in the forest instead of out of a van emblazoned JERRY HARPER, LOCKSMITH. 24-HOUR EMERGENCY SERVICE. BONDED.

He sat his toolbox down in front of the front door. "You were lucky to catch me. All three of my men are out on jobs. Yes, we keep real busy. Real busy. I was just out changing the locks on the house of a couple whose son's got to be a drug addict. He had already sold everything in the house—TV, VCR, everything."

"You mean they were locking their own son out of the house?" I asked. The thought chilled me.

"Yup." He took out his screwdriver. "We get a lot of calls like that. You'd be surprised. I don't know what the world's coming to. I've got four sons, all of them grown now and doing fine, and I say to them, 'What's happening to the world? What's gone wrong?' Nobody knows." He squeezed one eye shut and twisted the screwdriver. "Good for business, though, I have to say."

When he left, the brass of the new dead-bolt lock shone brightly against the gray wood of the door. Penn surveyed it with grim satisfaction. "If he wants to get in now, he's going to have to heave a cement block through the window and climb in, which I wouldn't put past him." Penn looked up at the sky and added grimly, "If it's going to rain, I wish it would go ahead and rain."

The rain felt like a blessing, as if it might wash away everything that was wrong. We ran around the house, shutting windows. Cold raindrops swept through the screens and against our faces. The wind threw the rain in sheets against the window. High up, it whined dangerously in the trees. Fast claps of thunder made us turn our heads sharply. Again and again lightning flashed an unearthly brilliance through the house. It seemed as if the heavens were exploding.

Penn puttered around barefoot in the kitchen, rattling pots and pans, opening and closing cabinets and the refrigerator, and at last the thunder grew more distant. He cooked creamed chipped beef on toast for supper. His mother used to fix that for him when he was sick, he said. We ate asparagus tips out of the can with our fingers, and then cold spiced apple rings out of the jar. Ovals of ruby encircled our mouths, and our fingers were sticky.

After supper I took a shower. When I stepped

out with a few strands of hair sticking in damp ringlets to my face, I glanced in the bedroom and saw that the sheets on the bed had been changed. Now they were jade green. Penn had been at work stripping any trace of Koo and Casey from the bed.

Fourteen

Dear Diary,

I wish we could have stayed at the cabin forever. We were so happy there! Why couldn't we stay?

Now we're back at school, and already my weekend with Penn is beginning to seem distant, the way a dream does in the morning. Our worry about Casey is setting our teeth on edge. I keep unconsciously bracing myself, but against what? I don't even know . . .

Casey might have dropped off the earth for all we had seen of him lately, but we knew where to find him. The window of the school's computer lab shone a pale blue-white rectangle whenever we happened to drive by the school at night.

"I can't talk to him," Penn told Stephen and Tessa at lunch on Monday. "I'm so mad at him, I'm afraid of what I might say."

"We can't let him stay off by himself all the time," Tessa said. "It's too dangerous."

"Hush!" I said, casting a nervous glance over my shoulder. Though we were accustomed to thinking of ourselves as alone in the crowded cafeteria, I lived constantly with the fear that someone might pass by our table at the wrong moment and hear what was being said. The thought made me so nervous that the sounds of the cafeteria, the clatter of trays, the hubbub of voices, became an indistinct swell of noise in my head like the roaring of the ocean.

"Don't worry," said Stephen. "Tessa and I will go by the computer lab tonight and get him to go out and eat with us. You know Casey. He can't pass up a free meal."

"That's a good idea," I said, relieved.

Penn rocked back in his chair. "Have you ever heard about the Einstein-Podolsky-Rosen paradox?" he asked.

"The EPR paradox?" ventured Tessa cautiously. "It has something to do with quantum physics, doesn't it?"

"Right." Penn smiled. "Dockerty was talking to me about it after class. The implications are incredible. What it comes down to is that if you disturb the quantum state of a particle, a photon, for example, it vanishes."

"I understand your thinking perfectly," said Tessa dryly. "If Casey were a quantum particle, our troubles would be over."

That evening Penn and I worked at the library until it closed at ten. Neither of us voiced the thought, but we were both worried about how Stephen and Tessa were getting on with Casey. Although it had been a strain letting Casey make a hog of himself at one expensive restaurant after another, I found myself almost nostalgic for those days. At least then his behavior had been fairly predictable.

The lights in the library's windows blinked, a final warning that the circulation desk was closing. We walked outside into the damp night air. Penn opened the door of the Corvette for me, then slid in behind the wheel.

He sat silently for a moment, staring ahead as our warm breath began to cloud the windshield.

A fat woman came out with a webbed plastic carryall full of books.

"I guess Stephen and Tessa could still be eating dinner somewhere," I ventured. "If they got a late start."

Penn didn't say anything, and finally I said, "You're worried about them, aren't you?"

"A little," he admitted. There was a long silence before he added, "Stephen can control his temper if he has to."

"Who are you kidding?" I said.

"No one, I guess." He glanced at me. "I don't much feel like going home yet, do you?"

"We could split a sundae somewhere," I suggested.

"Let's do that," he said.

As we drove off, I thought about how the car was its own world, as isolated as a ship at sea. The deeply slanted windshield, with its state inspection sticker a pale square in one corner, marked the farthest extent of my consciousness. In this small world, speeding along dark streets, I felt safe. Penn's hand lay lightly on my thigh under my skirt, but he was distracted, as if he were looking at something far away.

"What's wrong?" I asked abruptly.

Pulling away from me, he gripped the steering

wheel. "My dad found out about those bonds I cashed in. Somebody at the bank must have told him. He wanted to know why I suddenly needed so much money."

"What did you say?"

Penn shrugged. "I tried to be vague. Maybe I'd been a little extravagant, I said. Going out to dinner. Treating friends."

I smiled a little. "So what did he say? That money can't buy friends?"

"Hell, no. My father's no fool. He didn't believe me for a minute."

I sucked in my breath. "You told him the truth, then?"

"How could I?" His voice was unsteady, as if he were on the verge of tears. "Even if I wanted to, how could I? It's not just my secret. I couldn't tell him anything without telling him that Stephen and Tessa were there, that Stephen pushed Laurie off the cliff. I couldn't do that."

"So what happened?"

"He thinks I'm on drugs. He's made me an appointment with a substance-abuse clinic in Greensboro where nobody will know me. I had to promise him I'd go."

"What are you going to do?"

"I don't know," said Penn bleakly. "It's going to look bad for me when those blood and urine tests come up negative. I may have to take some drugs."

"Don't even joke about that."

"You think I'm joking? The only problem with that is if my dad decides to confide in one of his esteemed colleagues. And he may have done that already—he got that clinic's name from somebody. If it gets back to the police that I'm into drugs, guess who's going to become the number-one suspect in Laurie's death?"

"You've got to tell your dad you're a compulsive gambler," I said, gripping the armrest. "That would explain the money."

Penn burst out laughing.

"Is it that funny?" I asked, a little hurt.

He wiped his eyes. "No, I guess not. It's just that the whole situation is so bizarre. Sometimes I think I'm going to crack and end up in the same shape as Casey."

"Please don't do a striptease in the cafeteria," I said.

He smiled. "One thing's for sure—there's no way I can cash in another bond. Whoever my father's informant at the bank is, you can bet they'll be watching for that."

"Of course not," I mumbled. "That goes without saying. Your father is going to be watching you like a hawk."

Penn heaved a sigh. "I hope I can make Casey understand that."

I wasn't surprised when our route took us by the school.

"The computer lab is dark!" Penn said, glancing up at the window in alarm. "What do you think it means?"

I pointed out that all that showed was that Tessa and Stephen had taken Casey somewhere, which we already knew. Depressed, we drove to McDonald's and got a vanilla sundae and two spoons.

The restaurant was decorated with framed sketches of local points of interest—City Hall, the old cotton mill, the Falls. I averted my eyes quickly from the sketches. I had promised myself I wouldn't think of Laurie plummeting to her death, but it was impossible. Once I spotted the picture of the Falls, I could think of nothing else.

The place was over-air-conditioned and I felt gooseflesh rising on my arms and legs. I reached for Penn's hand, reassured by his warmth.

"Everything's going to work out," said Penn, sounding unconvinced. "Casey's probably getting over that MIT stuff already. Things could get back to normal."

I wondered how he defined normal. The police were investigating Laurie's death. Did he really think that was going to stop?

"Tell me what you think about all this," said Penn. "You're getting all quiet on me, and it's making me nervous."

I didn't have a chance to, because at that moment Stephen and Tessa burst in the door.

"Jeez! We're glad to see you!" Stephen slid in next to me and Penn moved over to make room for Tessa.

"We saw your car outside," said Tessa. "What an awful night!"

Penn's eyes met mine. We had our own reasons for being unhappy. I was already wondering how to break it to them that Penn was no longer in a position to buy Casey off.

Tessa's eyes widened. "We took Casey to the Pancake House. It was awful. Not too many people were there, but it's not like it was totally empty or anything, and Casey starts talking about—about—you know." She glanced anxiously around the restaurant.

"The accident," Penn interposed. "What happened?"

Tessa shuddered. "You know how Casey's voice carries. It was like he had a loudspeaker, Penn, no lie. He said he wondered if it was true that your life flashes before your eyes before you die, and had Stephen thought about that?"

Stephen gripped the saltshaker in both hands as if he were about to devour it. "He said he wasn't sure whether he believes it or not," he said tightly. "He said it made just as much sense for a killer's life to flash before his eyes as he did the deed, and what had been my experience with that?" The saltshaker fell. Stephen watched as it rolled around on the table in aimless circles. Penn stopped it with his hand and set it upright.

"He asked if I'd had a lot of nightmares since the—" Stephen choked.

"The accident," prompted Penn.

"That wasn't the word he used," said Stephen savagely. "And then he started on that law-and-order speech."

"He's parroting stuff he's heard other people say," said Penn.

"In the context," said Tessa, "it had a chilling effect. But that's not the worst part. At the next booth was a beefy guy who wasn't doing much eating. His pancakes were getting cold while he eavesdropped."

"He looked like an off-duty cop to me," said Stephen. "I was paralyzed. You can't imagine what it was like. Any minute I expected this guy in the next booth to whip out handcuffs, and Tessa and I had to be pretending to take everything Casey said as a good joke. Heh-heh."

Tessa's hands lay tightly folded on the table. Her nails were closely trimmed so the entire soft pink tip of the finger showed. "I wrenched the subject in another direction," she said, "by carrying on about what a genius Casey was and how geniuses are often not appreciated in their own time."

"Tessa was great," said Stephen. "She was sitting there flirting with Casey, the whole bit, batting her eyelashes, the delicate accidental touch of the hand." He grinned.

"I hardly even remember. It's all a blur," Tessa said rapidly. "I was so upset, I don't know how we got out of there."

"The worst part," said Stephen, "is that once we got out on the highway, I realized somebody was following us."

"Are you sure?" I cried.

"Of course I'm sure. I'll bet it was the guy in the next booth. I turned off at the Ivy Street exit and he turned right after us. Then I ran the red light at Ivy and Mason, and he ran the light, too."

"Maybe the light had changed by then," I said.

"I wish!" said Stephen. "I stepped on the gas, got around a corner before him, then backed up really quick into an alley."

"We were lucky we didn't wreck my car," said Tessa.

"Then we lay low. We were in the parking lot of an insurance company, I think."

"Casey thought it was a hoot," said Tessa. "He was in the backseat the whole time, laughing himself silly."

"Maybe he was drunk," said Penn.

"What difference does it make?" said Stephen impatiently. "The point is, drunk or sober, he's doing his best to land us in jail."

"Do you think this guy that followed you got your license number?" asked Penn.

"I don't know." Stephen glanced at Tessa.

"I don't think so," said Tessa. "Not as fast as we were going."

"We aren't going to keep on being lucky forever," said Stephen. "We've got to do something."

"Do you think we could persuade him to join AA?" I suggested.

They all looked at me as if I were an alien.

"It's a nice thought," said Tessa, "but I don't think Casey's problem is purely due to alcohol. He's also a little bit nuts, right?"

Penn glanced at me. "Joanna and I will go talk to him tomorrow night."

"Do yourself a favor," said Stephen, "and don't take him to the Pancake House."

Fifteen

. . . I'd love to grab hold of Casey and shake him until his teeth rattled. Who does he think he is? How can he treat us like this? Penn says Casey doesn't want to get us sent to jail. Maybe not, but can't he see that's where his crazy behavior is leading? We have to talk to him. Maybe he'll laugh at us, but it's worth a try. Isn't it?

A few lights shone along the baseboards of the open passageway to Haggerty, giving off a faint glow. It was eerie to be walking down the familiar hallway at night. The school buildings on the other side of the courtyard and behind us were large gray shapes in the dark. I could hear Penn breathing beside me.

"Whatever you do, don't start thinking about how Casey sneaked out to the cabin," I said. "That'll only make you mad."

"Don't think of a green polar bear," he responded.

I stifled my sudden laugh with my hand. Penn's teeth flashed white. His face was an indistinct pale smudge in the darkness. I rapped on the metal door of the lab.

"Who is it?" yelled Casey.

"Penn and Joanna," I said. "Would you like to go out and get a pizza or something?"

Air whooshed in my face as Casey whipped the door open. The glare from the sudden light made me blink. "Come on in," he said. "Too bad you didn't come by earlier. I already got Stephen to bring me a pizza."

A pizza box lay open on a filing cabinet, its corrugated interior sticky with tomato sauce and fragments of melted cheese. The closed blinds at the windows rattled in the breeze.

Penn glanced at the glowing computer screen but didn't say anything. I knew he was trying not to think about how Casey had sneaked out to the cabin.

"What are you doing?" I asked, glancing at the computer screen.

"Wouldn't you like to know?" Casey smirked.

Penn stiffened and took a step backward. "Well, if you don't want to get pizza—" he said, "I guess we'd better be going."

"Want to know what Dockerty's credit rating is?" Casey threw himself down in the plastic chair and surveyed the screen with satisfaction.

We moved closer to the screen and leaned over Casey's shoulders to peer at it. "What have you got there?" Penn asked.

"The files of the credit bureau," said Casey. "Can you believe Dockerty shops at Shop 'n' Save? No wonder his shirts look tacky. You'd be amazed what you can find out about people by reading their credit reports. But I've been doing other things, too. Last week it was banks." He punched some keys and the numbers on the screen went past our eyes with dizzying speed. The screen went blank, and with a few clunking noises, a set of numbers appeared. "I made a copy of these," said Casey. "Here's your bank balance, Penn. I didn't realize you were so loaded." He rocked back in the chair, balanced on its two metal legs. "Now that I know how much you've got stashed, I figure you could take us all on a Caribbean cruise. Wouldn't that be neat?" He cackled. "Hey, if you've got it, why not spread it around some?"

"If the bank's records are so clear to you, Casey," Penn's voice was icy, "you ought to be able to see that most of my money is in CDs. That's money my grandmother gave me to pay for college."

"Stin-gy!" cried Casey. "I've never seen such a stingy guy. You can cash in CDs, can't you? And there's plenty more where that came from. So what's the big deal about spending some on a vacation? We'll have a great time. I'd need a lot of new clothes, though. I hear they really dress up on cruises, dinner jackets, tuxedos, the works. Ladies dripping with jewels. Maybe we'll meet some beautiful spies. I can't wait." He clicked the space bar. "I went by the travel agency and picked up a bunch of brochures. Glamour, bikinis, and sunshine—va-voom! You know something, Penn? You don't understand the first thing about fun."

"Is that what you've been having with Koo?" said Penn coldly. "Fun?"

"You bet. There's a girl who knows how to party. Say, I've got an idea!" cried Casey. "Let's take Koo! The old bunch have gotten pretty stuffy, admit it! New blood is what we want."

Penn was so rigid he might have been stuffed by a taxidermist. After a quick glance in his direction, I scooted my chair up next to Casey. The metal legs of the chair scraped against the vinyl floor. "We haven't been seeing much of you lately, Casey," I said, wheedling. "We've missed you."

He looked gratified. "I've had a lot of important stuff to do. That's why. Breaking into computers takes more time than you'd think."

"It's like you're a modern-day wizard," I said. I had a momentary fear that my flattery was too obvious, but I needn't have worried. He poked out his thin chest complacently.

"The big thing was getting super-user status on the mainframe at State," he said. "This dinky unit here is no good by itself, but with State's hardware, it's easy. The best part is, I run every call through State's computer and then back here, so they'd have a heck of a time tracing me, even if they got onto me."

"Amazing!"

"They can still trace it, Casey," said Penn.

"Yeah, but it'll take 'em a while, and by then I'll be off the machine." The figures whirled past, and then the screen was blank. "I don't stay on any one line too long. Better safe than sorry."

"You know what?" I said. "We ought to do fun things together like we used to."

"Yeah. Like I said—a Caribbean cruise!" Casey smirked. "You're going to be crazy about Koo when you get to know her."

"I meant The Bakery!" I said quickly. "Now, we've really had some nice times there."

Casey pursed his lips. "You gonna tell me you'd rather go to The Bakery than to the Caribbean? Man, there's no comparison. The Bakery is dull. Just what you'd expect in this dull town." Abruptly he turned in his chair to face me. "You know, Joanna, I like you."

I blinked in surprise. "Thank you."

"But you're dull, too," he said. "What we all need around here is something to liven us up. I'll bring those brochures around to show you as soon as I get the chance. Yessiree! I would have done it before, but I've been too busy. I have to work at night, since that's when the banks are closed."

I was worried that any minute he would turn around and catch the murderous look in Penn's eyes. "You're so smart, Casey," I said hastily.

"Damn straight. But what I'm working on now is very, very tricky." His eyes narrowed as he stared at the screen. "Direct transfers. Banks do it all the time, moving money from one account to another electronically. What I've got to do first is persuade the bank computers that I'm a legitimate bank."

"But you aren't a bank!" I cried.

He grinned. "I'm not over at State, either. But the computer doesn't know the difference. Yessiree, this looks real promising. I'm already onto a lead or two, and I don't think it'll be too long before I figure out how."

"I think we'd better go, Joanna," said Penn quietly. "It's late."

"Don't run off," said Casey. "If you hang around, you might get to see my big break-through." He grinned broadly. "Watch me save Penn from his own selfishness," he said with a snicker. "It's kind of a Robin Hood stunt. Don't you love it?"

Penn pushed the door open with a sudden movement.

"We'll have to try you another time," I called to Casey.

I hurried down the passageway after Penn, our footsteps ringing on the cement. "Wait up," I said.

"Can you believe that?" Penn turned to me furiously. "He's sitting there telling me he's going to drain my bank account, and all the time he's got a stupid grin on his face!"

"Can he do it?" I asked.

"I don't know," said Penn shortly.

The Corvette was parked among the shadows on a service road behind the wing. Penn's keys flashed a sliver of light as he unlocked my door. Without saying a word, he walked around to the driver's side. His face was in the shadows, and I couldn't make out his expression.

A minute later he got in, bracing himself against the steering wheel with his hands. "Did you notice how I parked back here?" he asked. "It's farther to walk, but I like it because it's dark. I'm living like a fugitive already." He turned on the ignition, and the dashboard lights cast a faint glow on his face. "I keep trying not to be noticed," he said. "When I see a patrol car, I turn off on a side street to get away from it. I wonder if it's going to be this way the rest of my life."

"What are you getting at?" I cried.

He passed a palm over his forehead. "I don't know, Joanna. What am I going to do if Casey gets into my bank account? How does he think I could explain it to my dad if eighty thousand dollars in bonds evaporate into thin air?"

"Would you have to?" I asked. "I mean, it would be sort of like robbing a bank."

"That's for sure," said Penn.

"Wouldn't the bank make it good? I thought that was what Federal Deposit Insurance was for."

"What if he makes it look like I made the withdrawals myself?"

"He can't," I said. "Banks can always trace where the money went."

"Maybe," said Penn gloomily. "But even if they do, it's no good to me. If they trace it to Casey, there's no use expecting him to keep his mouth shut. He'll take all of us down with him."

"It can't be that easy to break into banks' electronic transfer systems," I argued. "Or people would be doing it all the time. Maybe we're getting upset over nothing."

"I hope," said Penn.

"I'm sure of it," I said.

The car's engine roared as he backed too fast out of the service drive. "What's got me scared," he said grimly, "is that when it comes to computers, Casey's a genius."

Sixteen

Dear Diary,

Penn's desperation is catching. I'm in a pretty bleak mood myself. It's awful to feel so helpless! All we can do is wait for Casey's next move. Penn has called his bank's 800 number a hundred times to check his balance. So far there's no sign that Casey has tapped into his account. But it could happen tomorrow, or even in the next five minutes.

It makes me feel dirty when I remember how I flattered him, Diary. I practically groveled at his feet. It seemed worth it at the time—anything to keep him from getting mad at us.

Casey is capable of doing almost anything. . . .

                    *   *   *

After physics class one day, I stayed behind to
ask Mr. Dockerty a question. Even though I had
missed out on the entire first semester of physics,
I was holding my own in class, thanks to Stephen
and Tessa's coaching. I still checked routinely to
make sure I understood everything. Dockerty answered my questions almost absentmindedly as
he shuffled papers on his desk. Abruptly he said,
"You're a friend of Casey's, aren't you?"

I was so taken aback, I couldn't speak.
Luckily he didn't seem to expect an answer. He
perched on the edge of his desk, and his round
glasses flashed with reflected light as he shifted
his position, giving him a curiously blank-eyed
look, "I'm worried about him," he said. "Does it
seem to you he's acting strange?"

I groped for a safe answer. "He's taking the
rejection from MIT pretty hard. Are you talking
about the striptease he did in the cafeteria?"

Dockerty shook his head. "I understood him
to say that was in the nature of a dare. No, that's
not what disturbs me. He's stayed after class
quite a few times lately—I have him the last period of the day, you know—to ask me questions
about spiritual matters." Dockerty took off his
glasses and polished them with an untucked bit

of his shirt. His lashless eyes blinked nearsightedly at me, bare and vulnerable, as if he were a mole puzzled by the light.

"What sort of spiritual matters?" I inquired cautiously.

Dockerty perched his glasses on his nose. "Life after death seems to be what preoccupies him most, I would say. He asked a lot of odd questions about God and outer space. That is a subject I try to steer clear of, living in the Bible Belt as I do." He sniffed. "I do not wish to be accused of robbing children of their faith. I repeated, as I always do when pressed on this issue, that religious faith is a subject outside scientific inquiry. But that didn't satisfy him. He was quite insistent. You know, Casey can be amazingly forceful."

"I know," I said. The clock on the wall clicked, but my gaze never left Dockerty's face.

"He wanted to know whether I believe there's such a thing as objective right and wrong and whether life is sacred." Dockerty's fingers drummed on his knee. "Really, I hardly knew what to say. I naturally began to wonder if he was thinking of doing himself harm, but I have to admit he never mentioned suicide explicitly. When I reflect on what he said, it seems to me there was an alarming lack of coherence. A few times he burst into an odd little set piece and began preaching on law and order."

I wondered how Casey fit his computer piracy into his law-and-order view of the world. Chances were he figured that the rules didn't apply to himself.

"I'm afraid I may have blundered." Dockerty coughed self-consciously. "I suggested he seek counseling. He seemed to take this as an affront, and he hasn't spoken to me since. I wondered if perhaps his friends—"

"He's not seeing as much of us as he used to," I said. "He's hanging out more with Koo Ambler these days."

Dockerty sighed. "No help there, I'm afraid."

"Do you really think he might be suicidal?" I heard the faintly hopeful note in my voice and blushed.

"I don't know. I must admit I am concerned. He seems morbidly preoccupied with religion." Dockerty cast a glance at his door, no doubt afraid a Bible-toting parent would burst in. "Not that there's anything wrong with that, but it seemed so unlike Casey." He frowned. "And so *irrational!*" he exclaimed.

I realized I was late to my next class. I had

been alarmed enough by Dockerty's words that I hadn't even heard the second bell ring.

"Let me write you an excuse," he said, reaching back into his desk drawer.

When he handed me the hall pass, he must have noticed how upset I was, because he added, "Maybe I'm making too much out of nothing, but I do think it might be helpful if one of his friends talked to him."

I nodded, and hurried out of the classroom.

At lunch I told the others what Dockerty had said.

"I can't stand it," said Stephen heavily. "That's all we need now—Casey gets religion. What a nightmare!"

"He's never been devout, has he?" asked Tessa. "He's never mentioned going to church."

"I think he's a Baptist," said Penn. "He went when he was little, anyway. I once saw one of those little checklists he brought home where you rate yourself: Have you read the Bible today? Have you tithed? That kind of stuff. You know how competitive Casey is—he gave himself a hundred percent."

"Casey reads the Bible every day?" Tessa asked incredulously.

"Sounds to me like he cheated," said Stephen.

"I don't think he's been to church in years," said Penn. "He's always home when you call him Sunday morning."

"All that stuff about life after death," said Tessa. "Could he be talking about ghosts? Do you think he can be having visions or hallucinations or something?" She looked around the table.

"If he's been sampling from those paper bags Koo stashed in my locker," I said, "it's perfectly possible."

"Casey on mushrooms!" Stephen winced. "I don't even want to think about it."

Penn leaned toward me. "Does Dockerty honestly think Casey might kill himself?"

"He seemed worried," I said.

"Wouldn't that be great?" Stephen closed his eyes. "No muss, no fuss, no bother."

"But how can he be planning suicide and a Caribbean cruise at the same time?" I objected.

"Maybe he plans to dive off the bow of the ship," suggested Stephen.

"Sometimes people make contradictory plans," argued Tessa.

"And, after all, nobody's claiming that Casey's making sense these days."

Stephen pressed his fingertips together and

smiled. "It's such a beautiful idea," he said, "that I'm afraid to look at it too closely for fear I'm going to see a logical flaw in it. Do you think there's any way we can help him along? How about if we send him some pamphlets from the Hemlock Society?"

"What about leaving Stephen's target pistol around?" suggested Tessa.

"Hi, you guys!" We all turned, conscience-stricken, to gaze at Nikki Warren. The edge of our table made pleats in her skirt where she leaned against it. She hugged a yellow legal-sized pad to her chest. Her cheeks were rosy, and her tiny gold earrings gleamed in her earlobes. She could have been an illustration in the *Girl Scout Handbook*. "I'm collecting suggestions for the senior-class gift," she said. "Got any ideas?"

We looked at her in stunned silence.

"Come on!" urged Nikki. "I was figuring you guys could come up with something creative."

Tessa closed her mouth. "Uh, what are some of the things other people have suggested?" she asked.

Nikki glanced down at her notepad, her expression guarded. "A new sign for the school. A new scoreboard." She paused.

"That's all?" I asked.

She frowned. "Some people are not taking this seriously. This is our class's chance to make a real difference around here, and all a lot of people can do is smart off about it."

"Gee, I don't know what to suggest," said Stephen. "This place is so perfect the way it is."

"That's exactly the kind of attitude I'm talking about," said Nikki sharply. "Remember, if you're not contributing to the solution, then you're part of the problem."

"I'm sorry," said Stephen, covering his face with his hands.

"A few tables outside, so we can get out of the cafeteria in good weather," I suggested desperately.

Nikki jotted it down. "I knew I could count on you, Joanna." She lifted her chin. "Some people think being cynical is funny, but it's only cheap." She flounced to the next table.

"The senior class could hire a hit man to get rid of Casey," muttered Stephen. "Now there's something that would enrich all our lives."

I glanced over to the next table. Nikki was writing quickly on her notepad. She was getting cooperation from one table, at least. "We've got to be more careful," I said. "Nikki could have heard us talking. We're acting as if we're in a protective glass bubble, but people are around us all the time. They could be listening."

Stephen was amused. "Look at you, Joanna! You're acting so sneaky, anybody would think you were plotting murder."

Seventeen

Dear Diary,

Can't the others see how close we're getting to murder? One minute we're talking about how neat it would be if Casey killed himself, how it would solve all our problems! And a minute later we're thinking about how we could help him along with it!

The truth is it isn't that much of a leap from wishing for Casey's suicide to actually killing him. Is it? What am I getting myself into?

I was working on physics at home that evening when Casey called.

"Joanna," he began.

It was so like Casey not to identify himself.

He expected me to know who he was. In fact, I recognized his voice at once, but that didn't keep me from being irritated.

"Come over to my house and get me," he commanded.

"Now?" I asked, astonished. "Is your car in the shop?"

"I wanna talk," he said. "Be here in fifteen minutes."

After I hung up, I stared at the phone for several minutes, seething. How peculiar that he had called me! He had never done that before. Distinctly uneasy now that I thought about it, I dialed Penn. To my relief he picked up the receiver. I was always nervous that I would get his father.

"Hullo?" said Penn.

"Casey just called me," I said. "He wants me to come get him. He says he has something he wants to talk to me about."

"Are you afraid to go alone?"

"No," I said. "Not really. He didn't sound exactly unfriendly. I don't know, though. There was something funny about his voice."

"He's probably drunk," said Penn. "When are you supposed to go pick him up?"

"Right now. He's expecting me in fifteen minutes."

"It's going to take all of that for you to get over there. Don't, I repeat, *don't*, let him drive. I don't like it, but you'd better go. We need to find out what's on his mind."

As I drove to Casey's house, I realized that the last thing I wanted to do was to hear what was on his mind. Every time Casey moved or spoke, we were wrenched this way or that. We had become sneaky, conniving, deceiving. It was as if he were making us over into his own image. And there was no escape. Next year Casey would be going to State right along with Penn and me. I could see him hanging around our necks there, talking loudly in the student union, humiliating us in public, milking us for money, demanding endless favors while we squirmed helplessly in his ever-tightening grip.

My car paused at the curb in front of Casey's house. A flush of pink tinged the horizon. The trees were inky-black silhouettes.

Casey lurched out his front door as soon as my car stopped. Smelling of dill pickles and beer, he got in the car, his red hair in untidy damp spikes and his pale face shiny. He sucked noisily on his finger. "Let's go to the Pancake House," he said. "I like the Pancake House."

I remembered Stephen's and Tessa's experience there. I had no intention of repeating their mistake. "Why don't we talk here?" I suggested.

"Because I want to get something to eat!" he said. "That's why. Don't start giving me that."

"We'll go to McDonald's, then," I said, turning the car around. "I'm not in the mood for pancakes."

"You're never going to get a husband if you're so bossy. You know that?" His narrowed eyes glittered venomously.

"I'm not worried," I said.

He squeezed my knee. "Plan to catch them with sex appeal, huh?"

I tried not to cringe at his touch. Fortunately it was not far to McDonald's. Moments later I pulled into the parking lot below the golden arches. As we went in, I got out my wallet and checked to make sure I had money. I had yet to see Casey pick up a check, and I was sure this little snack would be on me.

I had a peculiar cold feeling in the pit of my stomach, as if I were moving along a preordained path, about to collide with a train. Casey steadied himself against the counter and ordered a cheeseburger, fries, and a large shake.

"Let's go outside," I suggested, picking up his tray.

I opened the door, and Casey staggered through it before me and looked around in bewilderment. No wonder. Fat caterpillars of brightly colored plastic coiled through the air in several directions. By one slide a plastic figure wearing a pirate patch clung precariously to a tall plastic pole. Nearby a stout plastic tree grinned at us, its Bambi-large eyes startlingly clear in the dim light. A few small picnic tables were stationed among the slides and jungle gyms nearby so that parents could watch their children.

Casey fell heavily onto a seat. I unwrapped his cheeseburger for him, hoping that food would soak up the liquor in his stomach. He took a huge bite, and for a while he couldn't speak at all as he struggled to chew. Beads of sweat formed on his pale skin; his eyes bulged. It occurred to me that he might choke to death, but then he gulped suddenly and coughed. A bit of moist cheeseburger flew out of his mouth and landed on the table. I edged my hand away.

"I'm going crazy," Casey muttered. "Going around the bend, do you hear?"

"Would you like some black coffee?" I asked. "Black coffee is good if you—" I hesitated. "Well, anyway, black coffee is good."

He banged on the table with his fist. "No! I've got something to tell you!"

I congratulated myself on my foresight in making sure we sat outside. Fortunately, at this hour the playground was deserted. "You don't have to—" I began.

"I've got to tell you. You ought to know about Penn." He stared at me with glassy-eyed sincerity, and I suddenly had the awful feeling he had somehow got the impression I liked him. The thought made the smile freeze on my face. Suddenly Casey's hot palm was on top of my hand, trapping it. "You don't have a clue what really happened, do you?" he asked hoarsely. He snuffled wetly, and to my horror I realized tears were streaming down his cheeks, leaving shiny, crooked tracks. "You don't get it, do you? I'm telling you the truth—they murdered Laurie!"

I felt sick to my stomach, as if some overwhelming atrocity had been revealed to me. The little table put us knee to knee, and Casey's hot breath smelled ninety proof. I wondered vaguely if that was why I suddenly felt disoriented. Was it actually possible I was being poisoned by his breath? The bizarre, brightly colored playground equipment seemed to press

in on me, and I had the unnerving sensation
that if I turned around quickly, I would catch
the plastic figures moving.

I jerked my hand away.

"Did you hear me?" Casey repeated. "They
murdered her."

"Are you sure?" I said absurdly.

"Am I sure?" squealed Casey. "I was there. I
didn't have anything to do with it." He wiped his
snuffling nose with his hand. "Nothing whatever
to do with it." He looked up vacantly at the
giant plastic tree. "More sinned against than sin-
ning. Law and order—that's the ticket. I believe
in it." He blew his nose on a paper napkin and
then laid his head down on the table. "Jeez," he
mumbled. "It's unfair. I worked so hard, and
MIT—but anyway, I didn't have anything to do
with killing Laurie. I'm an innocent bystander.
Understand what I'm saying?"

"I think so," I said cautiously. "There was an
accident."

"Accident!" he shouted, suddenly sitting up
straight. "Stephen pushed her off the cliff. I'm an
eyewitness."

Only a white metal railing separated the playground from the parking lot around the restaurant. I began to have the morbid fear that

someone would get out of his car and hear what he was saying, yet something told me it would be a mistake to ask him to keep his voice down. He would probably shriek all the louder if I did.

I licked my dry lips. "Eat something, Casey. You'll feel better."

He balled up his fist and smashed it down on his cheeseburger, spewing ketchup in red spurts onto the table. "I could put Stephen's butt in the electric chair, you know that?" he said nastily. "All of them! I'll show them." He sniffled noisily. "No appreciation. After all I've done. Done everything for them. Every damn thing. And do they care? Pack of murderers. Stingy, too." Absentmindedly he picked up the flattened cheeseburger and took a bite. Ketchup dribbled down his chin, and bits of crumb clung to the corners of his mouth. I felt seasick, as if the playground were rocking violently.

Casey smiled nastily. "Shook you up, didn't I? That fancy car Penn drives. Those clothes. The pretty hair. Man, and all the time he's a murderer. Kind of gives you the creeps, doesn't it?" He shook his head with exaggerated slowness. "But nobody knows!" he hissed. "Nobody but them and me."

The door flew open with a whoosh that flut-

tered our napkins, and I looked up to see the
mountainous figure of Bobby Jenkins.

"I thought it was you out here," he said. In
the Lilliputian world of the playground, Bobby
looked like a giant. His hair was pulled back in
a ponytail, but clumsily so that damp strands
clung to his stubbled cheeks. His belly bulged
under a thin white T-shirt that had the sleeves
ripped off, and his worn jeans were white at the
seams and torn to expose one knee. "Need
some help?"

I froze, horrified, when I realized the potential
for disaster. What if Casey kept talking? "It's
okay," I said faintly. "Don't worry about us. I'm
going to get Casey a little coffee. He'll be fine."

To my relief, Casey had laid his head on his
hands again and was emitting a wheezy snore.

"He's drunk as a skunk," said Bobby. "What
do you say I carry him out to your car for you?"

"No, no," I protested nervously. "Really, it's
much better to let him sleep it off."

As if he hadn't heard me, Bobby hooked his
hands under Casey's arms and hoisted him over
his shoulder. "Hey, put me down," Casey demanded indignantly. "Lemme go."

With Casey over one shoulder, Bobby kicked
open the glass door and strode through the

restaurant. The neatly uniformed kids working at the counter stared as we passed. I had no choice but to trail unwillingly after them to my car. Jackknifed over Bobby's shoulder, Casey seemed to be having trouble catching his breath, which was just as well, under the circumstances. He was trying to say something, but it came out sounding like "oomph" and "onk." I unlocked the car door and let Bobby slide Casey inside. Casey wheezed and emitted a gargantuan burp. "You've got a nerve," he screamed. "If you just knew what I knew, you'd be sorry you're treating me this way!"

Hastily I slammed the door shut.

"Conceited little dweeb, ain't he?" Bobby asked, amused. "Jeez, I don't know how you can stand him."

"I guess I'd better be getting him home." I smiled uneasily.

Casey banged on the closed window with his fist. "Lemme out!" He pressed his pale lips against the glass and stared at us like some strange fish in a tank.

Bobby shook his head at the daunting sight. "It's enough to make a guy give up booze. Man, he's disgusting. I hope he doesn't puke all over your car."

Bad as that prospect was, it was by no means the biggest of my worries. I jumped in my car and sped out of the parking lot as fast as I dared.

When we arrived at Casey's house, the living-room windows had a dim bluish glow. The family was inside watching television. I wondered how I would get Casey inside without his parents' seeing the condition he was in. I went around and opened his door. "Leave me alone," he said thickly. "Don't you touch me." He slid out of the car and landed sitting on the street. As I watched helplessly, he braced his back against the car and shimmied up to a standing position. "Don't touch me!" he cried, throwing both his arms over the hood. "That Bobby's got a nerve. He makes me sick." He reeled suddenly, lurched away, and retched noisily behind a bush.

"Are you okay?" I asked.

"Sure," he said, tottering back toward me. "I'm fine. But I'm not going to eat any more cheeseburgers."

I watched him stagger up the front-porch steps. The door opened. I saw the faint bluish light of the television inside, and then the door closed. For some time I stood beside my car in a daze. Somewhere in the darkness a cat spat and yowled. A flutter of action stirred behind the bush, and a low dark shape rocketed across my line of sight.

Why had Casey told me? I wondered, feeling sick. Presumably the admiration I had flattered him with the other night in the computer lab had made him think I would be sympathetic, but there was a random recklessness about it that was frightening. Whom would he tell next? I was so upset, I had trouble laying hold of my car keys, but I forced myself to get back in the car and breathe deeply. I needed to get home and call Penn.

As I drove away, a roar drowned out the noise of my motor. I glanced in the rearview mirror and saw the leather-clad hand of a motorcyclist rise. The gloved hand moved slowly back and forth. My perception was so distorted that at first this struck me as an occult sign. Then the motorcycle passed me and with a start I saw that it was Stephen with a helmeted Tessa perched on the back of the bike. Penn's Corvette was almost on my bumper. The bike's right-turn signal flickered, and Stephen motioned me to follow.

Our vehicles stopped at a deserted playground next to an elementary school. Half-dazed, I got out of my car and joined the others. Someone had put an outsized tractor tire by the swings for children to play on, and Stephen and Tessa boosted themselves up onto it. I straddled a swing. An old-fashioned wooden seesaw was next to the tractor tire, and Penn sat there, his legs splayed out before him.

"Did you follow us to McDonald's?" I asked. A mosquito sang in my ear.

"Yes," said Penn. "I called Stephen, and he agreed we'd better trail you. Casey's been acting so strange, I didn't like to let you go off with him."

"We watched from the road," said Tessa. "The place is lit up, so we could pretty much see everything that happened without getting close. Penn was across the street behind a Dumpster. But we couldn't hear what you guys were saying."

"He told me," I said baldly.

"Just now?" gasped Tessa.

"I was afraid of that," said Penn.

My teeth chattered, and I couldn't speak for a moment. "Casey told me you were all murderers and that he was an eyewitness to the murder, and right then Bobby walked in."

"Oh, no!" cried Tessa.

"If Bobby finds out you killed Laurie," I said,

"he's going to kill you." I hugged myself tightly, trying to stop shaking.

We all sat for a long moment in silence.

"Do you think he's told anybody but you?" asked Penn finally.

Our eyes met. "I don't think so," I said. "He said, 'Nobody knows but me.'"

"Does anybody doubt," said Stephen between clenched teeth, "that Joanna is only the first of many to hear his ever-so-interesting story?"

"I'm surprised he hasn't told Koo," said Tessa nervously. "You know how he likes to look important."

"Casey may be acting crazy, but I think even he can see that telling Koo would not be smart. Talk about a loose cannon! She might make a public announcement." I snorted. "She might put it to music and sing it in the cafeteria. I wouldn't put anything past her."

"If he hasn't told her yet," said Penn, "he will. It's just a matter of time. I think they're getting very close." He hesitated, and I wondered if he was going to mention Casey's taking Koo out to the cabin, but he didn't.

"Did Casey say anything about turning state's evidence?" inquired Tessa anxiously.

I shook my head. "He kept saying he was an

innocent bystander and a witness to the murder."

"It would be a pleasure to get my hands around his neck," said Stephen in a low voice. "Can you believe it? He's the one that got us into this, and now he's got the nerve to say he had nothing to do with it."

"I think he hates us," said Tessa, surprised. "I've tried to be so nice to him, but underneath he must have always hated us."

"It's possible that he told Joanna," suggested Penn, "because he thinks she's safe. He must know she's not going to go to the police."

"But the police are going to get around to doing their routine on him pretty soon, wouldn't you think?" Tessa asked. "And now that he's spilled his story once, he'll probably be pretty quick to tell it again."

Stephen buried his face in his hands, and nobody said anything for some time. We could hear the faint hiss of traffic on the main road a block over.

"Couldn't he have an accident?" Tessa suggested.

"You mean, drink himself to death?" asked Stephen. "I don't think we can count on him to be so obliging."

"If we could only get him to lay off the

booze," said Penn, "maybe we wouldn't even have a problem. He might shut up."

"Don't you believe it," said Stephen. "The booze is the oil for his wheels, but the booze isn't the problem. Casey is the problem. And I don't know about the rest of you, but I don't intend to stand by and let him send me to prison."

"What exactly do you have in mind?" asked Penn quietly.

"It's us or him, Penn," said Stephen.

A dark car pulled up to the curb, and we all turned anxiously toward it.

"Jeez," whispered Stephen.

A shortwave radio crackled, and the blue light on the top of the patrol car flashed. The lights of the interior came on as a door opened and two uniformed cops got out.

"Police," a voice barked in the darkness.

A minute later I was dazzled by a bright light shining in my face.

"What are you kids doing out here at this time of night?" asked a gruff voice.

"N-nothing," said Stephen.

"We're j-just talking, Officer," said Tessa. Her face was a white caricature of itself in the strong beam of the big flashlight. Her mouth had fallen open and made a dark hole in the pale mask of her face.

The light scanned our clothes, capriciously spotlighting Penn's left hand, then Stephen's boots.

"Is that your car?" asked one of them, gesturing toward the Corvette.

"It's mine, Officer," said Penn.

"Let's see your driver's license, then, and your vehicle registration," said the other.

We waited in silence while the officer walked over to Penn's car with him.

When they came back, one of the officers said, "Don't you kids realize it's a bad idea to hang around these parks at night? You never know what kind of hoods you're going to run into. A very bad element hangs out at these places."

"Yes, sir," said Penn. "I guess we didn't realize how late it had gotten."

"Can we go now?" asked Tessa.

"Yeah, go on home," said the officer.

Penn walked with me to my car. "I'll call you tomorrow." His voice was wary. He glanced back toward the police car as Stephen's bike roared away.

"Penn," I said anxiously, "is it going to be all right?"

"You mean about Casey?" Penn glanced quickly at the police car. "I'll tell you the truth, love—I don't know."

> . . . *I didn't really want Penn to tell me the truth. I'm sick with nerves; I need to hear a comforting lie. What if Casey had fingered Penn right there in front of Bobby? He came so close! He's told me; he tried to tell Bobby. Who is he going to tell next? Even thinking of it makes me freeze in horror.*

Eighteen

The next morning I got up and dressed for school as if I were in a trance. It was Thursday and my father was out of town at a conference. When I pulled up the blinds, I could see a maintenance crew from the golf course driving a little blue tractor with black rubber rollers in front. A crow flew low over the lake. A strangely passive feeling had come over me. I think on some insane level I believed that Penn and the others were hard at work on our problem, and that meant everything would be all right.

I drove to school and got my books out of my locker. Koo and Casey, luckily, were not around. Dockerty showed the class a video about the origins of the universe. On the television screen, stars formed and collapsed into black holes, galaxies rotated into twin-lobed shapes and shot out radio waves, space and time were curved. In such a vast context, my troubles seemed small.

When I got to the cafeteria, I spotted Penn across the crowded room. My eyes searched his face as I drew closer, but I saw no clue there about what he was thinking.

"Is everything all right?" I asked anxiously. I sat down.

"I guess. So far no police are around."

"Have you seen Casey yet?"

"No." Penn rubbed his eyes. "Maybe he didn't even make it to school today. I wish I'd slept in myself. Stephen and I were up till two or three trying to think of foolproof ways to get rid of Casey. I think we got pretty punchy, because when I finally got up this morning, a lot of the things we were saying seemed crazy. I had this weird feeling I'd better go straight over to Stephen's and make sure he wasn't working on extracting poison out of hibiscus flowers."

Stephen and Tessa brought trays of cafeteria food to the table. I was astonished to see Tessa's plate heaped with pink spaghetti. I suppose it was a measure of how upset she was, because she hated cafeteria spaghetti.

"Have either of you seen Casey?" I asked them.

"Let's don't talk about Casey," said Tessa, her voice rising shrilly. "Not here."

"I haven't seen him." Stephen sat down and stirred his spaghetti disconsolately with his fork. "If there's any justice in the world, he's sitting at home in a dark room nursing a hangover."

"That's true," said Penn, brightening.

The thought that Casey might be out of the picture, even if for only a day, cheered us all.

After school Penn came by my house to pick me up. "Let's go over to Stephen's," he said. "Tessa's there."

I got in the car. "They aren't working on extracting poison from hibiscus, are they?"

Penn laughed.

Stephen's family lived in a two-story white colonial hedged with holly bushes. A wreath made of a pleated flower print sat primly on the front door. Nobody answered our knock, so we went in. The inside of the house featured a neat formal living room and a small dining room, but clearly neither of these rooms was used much. Behind the front rooms lay the comfortable living quarters of the house—a generous den, kitchen, and family room, the walls paneled in some dark wood, a big brick fireplace, chairs slip-covered in a wagon-wheel print. A hooked rug lay before the television set, and magazines and newspapers were heaped on the table. A pair of jogging shoes, one turned top down, lay by the lamp. There was no sign of Tessa and Stephen, but at last we found them downstairs in the dimly lit basement rec room. They were playing Ping-Pong. Penn closed the door at the top of the stairs when we came in.

"You can leave the door open if you want," Stephen said carelessly. "Mom, Dad, and Karen have gone to Tysonville for a nice visit with Auntie Maude and her brood of horrible kids." The ball hit the green table with a sharp crack and then bounced off Tessa's racket with a hollow pock. The alternating *crack-pock, crack-pock* rhythm continued like a peculiarly nerve-racking drumbeat.

"I've been telling Joanna about our research into untraceable poisons," said Penn.

"Laugh," panted Stephen, leaping for a ball, "but do you have a better idea?"

Penn draped his long legs over one arm of a tattered overstuffed chair. On the wall was a large, circular dartboard. He carelessly lobbed a dart toward it. It hit the bull's-eye and quivered there a second. "Maybe we ought to take our chances at a trial," Penn said.

"Damn!" cried Stephen. He looked down. A crushed white ball was under his heel.

"Game," said Tessa.

Stephen fell into a chair. "I get it." He turned to face Penn. "We act guilty as hell, hide the body, forge a letter to throw them off the track, and then we say it was all a mix-up and that really we're innocent."

"Okay, we made some mistakes," admitted Penn.

"We gave Casey a knife to hold to our throats," said Stephen bitterly. "That's what we did. He can say we're murderers, and because we acted like murderers, everybody is going to believe him."

Tessa threw down her paddle. Her damp hair clung to her temples, and her mouth was slightly open. "Penn, you mean to tell us that you really think we'd have a chance of getting off?"

"With Casey perjuring himself, don't forget," put in Stephen.

Penn's hands opened helplessly.

The phone rang with a loud clangor, and Stephen reached for the receiver. "Hullo?"

We all watched in suspense as he held the receiver, saying nothing. Finally he said, "Now?" He hung up without saying good-bye. "Casey wants me to bring him a pizza. Now."

"Why doesn't he just have one delivered?" I asked.

"He'd have to pay for it himself then," Tessa said.

Stephen tossed his Ping-Pong paddle onto the table. It wobbled and fell with a clatter. "It's not the money. It's a sick power thing. He wants to make me jump. I bet I've taken pizzas over to him five times. The guy could be a poster child for junk food. But what can I do? The point is, he *can* make me jump."

"I think we ought to try to reason with him," said Penn. "Maybe he doesn't understand where this is leading."

"Oh, he understands it, all right." Stephen combed his fingers through his hair. "Nobody ever said Casey was stupid. He's probably figuring he'll love being the star witness at our murder trial!"

We picked up the pizza; I held the warm box in my lap as we drove. Stephen's bike roaring ahead of us was so loud it blotted out all thought. As we drove past streetlights and neon signs, a kaleidoscope of color and light flashed through the car. The noise and the shifting light were disorienting. It was hard to believe we were driving on the same streets we had driven on countless times before. Everything looked different, and I had a curious floating feeling.

A garish neon sign gave Penn a red halo, and for a fraction of a second I caught my breath at the sight. "We could leave here," I said suddenly. "We could get on the interstate and keep driving."

He glanced over at me. "Are you having a panic attack?" he asked.

"Yes." The roar of the bike sounded distant now.

Penn put his hand at the back of my neck and squeezed. I knew he was trying to help me relax, but at the speed we were going, I wished he would keep both hands on the wheel.

Light glowed in the computer lab's window when we arrived. Penn pulled up in the shadows of the back service road, and I got out with the pizza. Stephen's bike was parked next to the loading-zone sign. Clad in leather gloves and jackets, Tessa and Stephen were all but invisible.

Only the whites of their eyes and the gleam of their helmets showed in the shadows.

> *. . . Terror swept over me in the parking lot, Diary. I thought that maybe we should turn back. Somewhere in my mind, I knew that something terrible was going to happen. . . .*

"Ready?" asked Tessa softly.

Even though panic was fluttering in my throat, I found myself walking along with them. Someone's sneakers made a squeaking noise as we trudged down the passageway of the wing. "Pizza," Stephen called. He banged on the door of the lab.

"Enter!" yelled Casey grandly. His eyes glittered as we all filed in. "What's this?" he asked. "A delegation? Put the pizza right there, folks, on that filing cabinet. I wish you'd gotten the party size. I didn't know we were going to have a mob here tonight."

"It's okay," Penn said, glancing at the others. "We aren't hungry."

We stood bunched close to each other, near the door, as if we were planning to escape the first chance we got.

Casey reached into the box and took out a slice of pizza. "I said double cheese!" He frowned. "You forgot to tell them double cheese."

"Sorry," said Stephen curtly.

"You'd think you could remember a simple pizza order," said Casey. He sprawled in his chair. "You guys came by at a pretty exciting time. I've figured out how to identify myself as a bank. I could be minutes away from being able to drain bank accounts at will." He smiled. "Cool, huh?"

"Casey," said Penn evenly, "it's hard enough explaining to my dad how I'm going through hundreds of dollars a month—he's convinced I'm on drugs. He's already set up an appointment at a clinic for me. How do you think I'm going to explain the disappearance of all that college money?"

Casey gave him a sly sideways glance. "Maybe you won't need all that money."

"What do you mean by that?" asked Tessa anxiously. "What are you getting at, Casey?"

"You guys have some problems with the police, don't you?" asked Casey. "I thought you might have to ask for—what do they call it?—deferred admission. If you get locked up, I mean."

"Casey, how can you talk to us that way? I thought we were your friends." Tears welled up in Tessa's eyes.

"Don't plead with him, Tess," snapped Stephen. He peeled off his leather jacket and tossed it to the floor. It clunked against the vinyl.

"What's that?" cried Casey, alarmed. "Why does it make that sound?"

Stephen blanched. "No big deal. It's just my new toy."

Casey leaned over and hooked the jacket with his free hand.

"Leave it alone, Casey!" cried Stephen. "It's none of your business."

"Ha-ha!" gloated Casey. He groped in the pockets. "What do we have here?" He fished out a black metal gun. It was Stephen's target pistol. Instinctively I pressed myself against the wall.

Casey stared at Stephen wonderingly. "What the heck are you up to, Steve, old bean?"

"The question is, Casey, old bean," said Stephen sarcastically, "what are you up to? If you think you're going to cut a deal with the cops, you're living in a dreamworld. We're sick of putting up with you, you know? You want to go to the police? Go ahead. I can't go on jumping every time you raise a finger. You're a blackmailer, pure and simple. Well, I'll tell you something." Stephen took a step toward Casey. "I'd rather spend my life in jail than live with you hung around my neck."

I heard Penn's quick intake of breath behind me, but I did not turn around. My frightened gaze leapt from Casey to Stephen and back again.

Casey's face had turned an unbecoming red. "I may be a blackmailer, but at least I'm no murderer. Okay, I will talk to the police. See how you like them apples, your majesty."

The gun was in Casey's hand and was pointed at Stephen, which may have accounted for his bravery. I was light-headed with fear. I saw a sudden movement to my right, and almost before I knew what had happened, Stephen lunged at Casey. An explosion rang out and Casey slumped. I must have screamed. I know my ears were ringing and my throat felt raw as I watched the pistol fall to the floor with a clunk.

"Is he dead?" cried Tess shrilly.

Casey's head was thrown back, and a shiny black spot glistened under his chin. Penn laid his fingers along the white column of Casey's neck. "Yes," he said flatly. "He's dead."

I heard Stephen laugh unsteadily. "L-looks like Casey committed suicide."

"Don't anybody touch anything," said Tessa. She was putting on her gloves. Her face was beautiful and blank, like the face of a marble statue.

Suddenly sick, I turned around and groped for the doorknob.

"Don't touch it!" cried Penn.

"I'm going to be sick," I said.

Penn wrapped a handkerchief around his hand and twisted the knob. I staggered outside and leaned against the railing. The cool night air pressed against the pulsing heat of my face. I pressed my fingertips to my throbbing temples. I felt so sick, I was able almost to forget the terrible scene in the room directly behind me. It seemed unreal, as if I had blinked three times and turned around, it would turn out to be a mistake. I wondered vaguely if Penn could be right about Casey's being dead. Could someone die as quickly as that? Shouldn't we at least try to do CPR or something? But then I realized that the bullet must have exited through the top of Casey's head. That meant it would have gone right through his brain. He was dead.

I felt Penn's warm arm around me. "Are you okay?" he asked.

I grabbed his hand and held on tightly.

A whispering noise sounded behind me, and I turned around quickly in a panic, but it was only Tessa. Her movements were oddly jerky, and the whites of her eyes showed. "Stephen was wearing gloves," she whispered. "Has anybody else touched anything?"

"Tessa." I looked at her. "You're whispering."

She held a finger up to her lips. What difference did it make whether we were quiet? I thought wildly. Casey can't hear us.

"As long as our fingerprints don't show up on the doorknob on top of Casey's, we're okay," Penn said impatiently. "Any of us could have been in the computer lab perfectly innocently, so it doesn't matter if we touched anything else. Let's get out of here."

He guided me toward the car; I must have been in shock. But when we got to the car, I looked around as if I had suddenly regained consciousness. I remember being glad that it was dark on the service road. Nobody could see me, really. I didn't have to try to look normal. Penn unlocked my door. "We have to hope nobody saw our car," he said. "The sooner we get away from here, the better."

"Are we going to leave him there like that?" I

asked, when Penn got in. "Shouldn't we call an ambulance?"

"He's dead," said Penn, turning on the ignition. "An ambulance isn't going to change that."

Tessa's face appeared at Penn's window. Lit from below by the dashboard lights, she had an evil expression, and I shivered. She fastened the strap on her helmet. "If we all stick together," she whispered, "and if nobody has seen us here, we ought to be all right."

"We'd better leave in different directions," said Penn. "I'm going to go without my lights until I'm clear of the school."

Tessa nodded.

I glanced behind as we drove off and saw their helmets gleaming, close together by the bike. Their jeans and black leather jackets were lost in the shadows.

"Why is she whispering?" I asked.

"It's probably shock," said Penn.

The Corvette slipped quietly away. In moments we were a block away from the school. I heard Penn exhale as he flipped on the headlights. "I haven't seen any other cars, have you?" he asked.

I shook my head. "Penn?"

He glanced at me.

"Was it—an accident?" I shivered.

Penn hesitated. "Sure," he said.

. . . Penn was lying. I'm sure I know that. What happened when the gun went off was confusing. We were all standing close together and everything happened so fast—a movement too quick to comprehend, an explosion, and then suddenly everything was different. What I can't get out of my mind, Diary, is seeing Stephen's black-gloved hand, its fingers wrapped around the gun's butt. Stephen had to have pulled the trigger! That gun didn't go off by accident.

Rain had begun to fall. I could hear it lightly and steadily striking the windshield, like tapping fingers. Beads of red gathered on the windshield, reflecting the ruby taillights of the car ahead of us. "I think it will be all right," Penn said. "Stephen had gloves on, so there's no gunpowder on his skin, even if they test for that, and they won't. It will probably pass for suicide."

"Casey would never have killed himself," I said. Funny how sure of that I was now.

"He practically did," said Penn grimly. "You know yourself that he was asking for it. Anyway,

Tessa thinks it's worth a try to make it look like suicide. She put on Stephen's gloves and typed 'I can't bear it anymore' on the computer screen. We'll have to see what the police make of that. We pushed the lock in and let the door swing shut behind us, so it'll look as if he was alone. Dockerty will swear he was depressed about being turned down by MIT and that he was asking about whether there was life after death." Penn snorted. "Imagine asking Dockerty a question like that!"

"What about the gun?" I asked.

"It was Stephen's gun," Penn admitted. "There's no getting around that. But Stephen can explain that he used it for target practice."

"Plenty of evidence for that," I said thinly. "All those bullet holes in the outhouse."

"Right. Stephen can say that Casey stole it." Penn glanced at me. "Are you okay?"

"I guess." I shivered.

"We should go someplace and try to act completely normal," Penn said.

"Isn't it rather late to be thinking about an alibi?" I asked. On second thought, I realized that it was probably a good idea. "We could go to the donut shop," I suggested.

"Poor Casey," said Penn unexpectedly.

I groped in my purse for a tissue and blew my nose.

"Funny, isn't it?" said Penn. "Now that he's dead, I've started remembering the good things about him."

I sniffled. "I guess that happens. That's why they say 'the dear departed.'"

"I can't do it," Penn said.

I stared. Had he decided to go to the police after all? "Do what?" I asked numbly.

"Buy donuts." A muscle in his jaw jumped. He turned the car sharply, and I heard brakes squeal behind us. A horn blew. "I can't act normal," he said. "I have the creepy feeling that if I go into Donut King, it's going to turn out there's blood on my shoes or something."

Involuntarily I glanced at his feet.

"I've already checked them." Penn grimaced. "I guess we should go home and go to bed."

When we reached my house, Penn leaned over me to throw the door open. I started to get out, then suddenly thought better of it and threw my arms around his neck. "I love you," I whispered.

We clung together for a moment. Then Penn let his fingers slide down my cheek. "We'll get through this somehow." He struggled to smile. "We've got to."

*   *   *

... I handed Casey antacid tablets wishing they were poison. I crossed my fingers and wished he would put an end to his life. But now that he's dead, I can't seem to grasp the finality of it. It's as if he left town and is expected back at any minute. But I know that's not going to happen. ...

Nineteen

Dear Diary,

Funny thing. I used to have a lot of trouble sleeping, but last night I fell asleep as soon as my head hit the pillow. Murder is a pretty extreme cure for sleeplessness, but it looks like it's a hundred percent effective. Maybe I fell into unconsciousness because there was so much I couldn't face. I don't know.

When I woke up this morning, it took me a few seconds to remember what we did last night. Then it hit me: We'd killed Casey.

I mean, Stephen killed Casey. We'd all talked about it, but it was Stephen who brought the gun along. He's the one who pulled the trigger. He's the one who's really guilty, right?

But we've been covering up for Stephen.
We're all in it together. Isn't that just as bad
as pulling the trigger?

No! It's not the same. I'm not a mur-
derer.

I feel tired. So tired! My limbs are heavy,
as if I were filled with novocaine.

I was in a fog the entire morning. I scarcely thought anything about it when I drove into the school parking lot and saw that it was empty, an acre of black asphalt. I couldn't stop myself from glancing up at the window to the computer lab. A movement there made me jump, but it was only the blinds being blown by the breeze from the open window.

The sound of a motor made me turn my head. Penn's Corvette pulled up beside me, and he jumped out. "I called you," he said, "but you'd already left. We forgot that today is a teacher workday."

I looked at him blankly. It was Friday. "You mean Casey's going to be left in there until Monday?"

Penn frowned. "Maybe the cleaning crew will find him. Look, we've got to get away from here. Let's go to the Pancake House. Have you had breakfast?"

*   *   *

Inside the Pancake House the smell of sausage and bacon mingled with the strong smell of cigarette smoke. At the counter an obese man with sideburns dug into grits and sausage. When he raised his fork, his shirtsleeve slipped up to reveal a bulging upper arm and a blue tattoo with MOM framed in hearts and flowers.

"Funny," said Penn, "that you never see a tattoo that says Dad."

The waitress laid our plates down before us and bustled off. Steam rose from our untouched eggs. Penn leaned over the table, so close to me that I could feel his breath. "Casey's mom called me this morning wanting to know if I had any idea where he could be. Last night they checked with the highway patrol and the local hospitals."

"Maybe you ought to suggest she get the police to break into the computer lab," I said.

"I don't think that would be such a good idea. I don't want to sound as if I know too much."

"You'd think she'd come up with that idea herself. He practically lives—" I paused uncomfortably, then corrected myself. "He practically lived over there."

"Well, at this point they're thinking he may have had a car accident." Penn said. "I figured it was best to act like I didn't have any idea where he could be. I gave her the names of a few other people she could call."

The waitress reappeared to freshen our coffee. She stared at our untouched plates. "Something wrong with the eggs?" she asked.

"No." Penn smiled at her. "Everything's fine."

"Eat it before it gets cold." The waitress bustled off.

"Eat," Penn said.

I ate. I put forkfuls of food in my mouth, chewed and swallowed, but I felt as if I were going to choke. Unable to bear another bite, I wrapped my cold toast in a napkin and thrust it into my purse.

Penn laid a tip beside his plate, then got up and paid the check. We drove to City Lake, a favorite local picnic spot. We parked on the circular drive that surrounded the lake, and I tore my toast into bits and threw it out on the water. The toast drifted on the ripples and began to sink. Ducks squabbled over it, pecking at each other. Suddenly a motorcycle roared up, and the ducks fled in a wet flurry of wings.

Tessa slid off the back of the bike. "Tessa's got laryngitis," said Stephen. He turned toward us, his helmet dangling from his hand by its strap. He reeked of gas fumes and smoke. His loose cap of dark hair shone in the morning light as he looked down, groping in his leather jacket for cigarettes and matches. "We called you both," he said, striking a match. "But nobody was home, so we went out looking for you." He smiled crookedly and took the lighted cigarette out of his mouth. "I guess we don't want to be alone."

"Maybe we could all go to the cabin for the weekend," whispered Tessa. "Get away."

Penn tore a bit of grass from the bank. "I don't think that would be a good idea. We ought to hang around town this weekend, making sure everybody sees we're acting normal."

Stephen inhaled deeply. "I don't feel normal. I feel like hell."

"Maybe we ought to call Casey's house and ask for him," whispered Tessa.

The idea was so macabre that I started.

"Now that would be abnormal." Stephen snorted. "I can't remember the last time I called him."

"The problem is," said Tessa sadly, "I can't remember what normal feels like."

Stephen tossed his cigarette to the ground. Its orange coal glowed on the grass. "D-does anybody believe in g-ghosts?"

We all stared at him in alarm.

"Don't look at me like that," he said irritably. "All I did was ask a simple question."

A carroty flash caught our eye, and we all turned and stared at a redheaded child bicycling around the drive. He was whistling through his teeth. I was relieved to see that he was only about ten years old. His braces flashed in the sunlight.

Penn took a shuddering breath. "Of course there's no such thing as ghosts. When you're dead, you're dead."

Stephen raked his hair out of his eyes with his fingers. "Do you know sometimes, when you have trouble sleeping, how you can't tell what's real from what isn't?"

I nodded sympathetically. I knew precisely what he was talking about. Since I had found out about Laurie's death, I had spent many sleepless hours tossing and turning, fighting horrible nightmares.

"I've got some sleeping-pill samples at home," said Penn. "Do you want me to get you some?"

"Nah," said Stephen. "I'll be all right." He tapped the pack against his hand and shook out another cigarette.

An ancient Volkswagen, heavily repainted

with peace signs, hearts, and quotations, puffed around the circle and zipped up beside Penn's Corvette. Koo climbed out. She was bursting out of the bodice of her tightly buttoned dress, which was of a sheer yellow flowered gauzy material. "Do any of you guys know where Casey is?" she asked.

"No," said Penn. "His mother called me wanting to know where he was, but I figured maybe he was with you."

Koo frowned. "You know, something about this gives me the creeps. I'm starting to get worried."

"You think he's been in a car accident?" whispered Tessa hoarsely.

"What's wrong with her?" asked Koo.

"Laryngitis," I said.

"No, he hasn't been in a car wreck," said Koo sarcastically. "If you're in a car wreck, the cops are on the scene, like, instantly. Unless you drive your car right into the river and nobody sees you crash." Her eyes narrowed. "You know, when you think about it, this is really weird. First Laurie disappears, and now Casey."

We were all struck dumb by her artless comment.

"Boy, you guys are a barrel of laughs," complained Koo. "Don't you ever talk?"

"You're scaring us with all this talk about Laurie's murderer lurking," I said.

"Stands to reason the murderer's around somewhere." Koo shrugged. "I know the cops thought Bobby killed her, but he didn't."

"How can you be so sure?" Stephen thrust both hands in his pockets and puffed energetically on his cigarette.

"Because I know him," Koo said. "Bobby wouldn't kill a girl."

I could feel goose bumps rising on my arms. Heavy in the air was the implication that Bobby would think nothing of killing a guy.

"Maybe Casey's left town and hasn't mentioned it to anybody," said Penn.

"Yeah," Koo said derisively. "Yeah. Sure. That's what they said about Laurie."

We all watched speechless as she lifted her skirts and climbed into the Volkswagen. Making a noise like a lawn mower, it sped away.

"I wish to hell somebody would find Casey's body," said Stephen. He ground the cigarette stub under his heel.

The next day Penn went over to Casey's house and sat with the family. He felt since he was one of Casey's oldest friends that he had to give his support to Casey's family. I whipped through the Sunday paper until it was strewn all over the kitchen, but I hadn't the faintest idea what I had read. My eyes were drawn again and again to the daisy-shaped clock on the wall. I washed and ironed everything I owned. The hiss of the iron and the warmth that rose from the ironing board was a comfort to me, and the repetition of the simple task was soothing. The metal prow of the iron whined as I drew it over my twill skirt.

Late in the afternoon, when the shadows were long, Penn appeared at the front door. "Mrs. MacNamara has called the police," he reported. "Casey's dad is away on a business trip, but he's flying home."

"Nobody has thought about looking in the computer lab yet?" I darted an anxious glance across the street to where Bobby's car was parked.

"No," said Penn. "Not yet. Do you want to go get something to eat?"

"Sure." I grabbed my wallet off the couch. As I slid into the Corvette's seat, I glanced over at him. "So, I guess it was pretty bad over at Casey's house."

"Yes." The car shot out of the driveway. Penn looked so distracted, I wasn't sure he even saw the road ahead. "Casey's mom kept pointing out to me that Laurie's killer is still loose."

"She thinks Casey's been murdered?"

"Yes. But she also clings to the hope that he's wandering around in an amnesiac haze, and that her 'darling boy' will come home to her."

"Oh, Penn!"

"This is not a day I would live over, for anything in the world," said Penn, gripping the steering wheel tightly.

I touched his cheek lightly, but his face remained blank and he continued to stare unseeing at the road ahead.

When I saw Penn getting out of his car on Monday morning, I ran over to him and buried my face against his chest. I didn't want to let go of him. Finally he murmured in my ear, "Hey, we're supposed to be acting normal, remember?" Startled, I pulled away. He was smiling down at me wryly. A muscle twitched at the corner of his eye.

Together we gazed at the window of the computer lab. The slanting rays of the sun had turned all the windows on the wing to bronze, and I couldn't tell if the blinds were still drawn or not. I sucked in my breath. "No, nothing's different," said Penn. He enveloped my hand in his, and we began walking toward the buildings. I glanced over at him. The close-cropped hair in front of his ear glittered in the morning light. His blue eyes were shadowed, as if they had sunk more deeply into their sockets. I was shocked at the shiver of fear I felt at this sign of vulnerability. Had I secretly hoped Penn would take care of me?

"I had a dream last night," he said, "which is kind of strange, because I never dream."

Kids went past us, laughing. They must have been in the band, because one of them, a tall skinny boy, had a pair of wooden drumsticks tucked in his belt.

"It wasn't scary or anything like that," said Penn, looking puzzled. "Casey was just standing there."

I squeezed his hand.

"It was good to see him," said Penn simply.

This morning the school buildings seemed unreal to me, as if they were made of flat canvas and could be rolled up. The illusion was so powerful that when we passed the administration building, I dragged my fingertips along the roughness of the brick and mortar to reassure myself that it was solid.

We rounded the corner and found ourselves facing Bobby, who was sitting, feet dangling, on the edge of the raised-brick flower bed at the side of the building. "I hear Casey didn't come home this weekend," he said.

Penn pulled me closer and wrapped his arm around my waist protectively. "We're all pretty worried about him," I said.

Bobby lifted his shaggy head to look at us. "Maybe he's dead. Maybe we're all gonna get picked off one by one, and they'll end up calling this place the high school of the damned."

Penn pressed his fingers against the small of my back to hurry me on. A moment later he glanced over his shoulder uneasily. "Do you think he's drunk?" he asked.

"No," I said. "I think he is upset."

When we passed Haggerty, we glanced briefly down the passageway to the door of the computer lab, then looked away guiltily and hurried past. I pressed my cool fingers against my closed eyelids for a moment. The school seemed unusually noisy. "Someone will have to find him soon," said a voice.

I turned to Penn in alarm. "Did you say something?"

"No." He squeezed me. "It's all right. You're not going crazy. It's just nerves."

"Hey, you guys!" A boy wearing a baseball hat turned backward was calling to us. He was sunburnt and his pants hung so low that an inch of white underwear showed at the belt. "Somebody says Casey's car is parked down by the Dumpster at the end of Haggerty."

We froze. "We'd better go," Penn said.

We avoided the hallway that would take us past the room where Casey's body lay. Several groups of kids were going in the same direction. I hadn't thought about it before, but since Casey ran the computer lab, practically everyone knew who he was. His striptease in the cafeteria had given him even more fame. More people than I would have guessed were disturbed by his disappearance.

I was surprised and oddly touched to see that Mr. Dockerty was walking just ahead of us. His gray slacks were shiny on the seat, and the button was missing on his sagging back pocket.

The Dumpster was on a short road that branched off the utility road behind the building. A small crowd had already gathered around Casey's car. The little blue car was so poignantly evocative of Casey that I almost burst into

tears—the bumper sticker with a drawing of a
naked woman, the crumpled cellophane corn-
chip package and cookie crumbs sticking to a
puddle of melted ice cream under the rear window, an empty package of computer diskettes on
the backseat. Dockerty peered underneath the
car. "The car was obviously parked here before
Thursday night's rain," he commented. "There
are no marks of rain on the dust under the car."

A slow chill crept up my spine. For a panicky
instant I had the sensation that Dockerty had
watched us that evening. I had to remind myself
that he couldn't possibly know what had happened.

A scream rent the air. Penn shuddered and
involuntarily glanced over his shoulder. Dockerty
took off running. The pack of kids thundered
after him, and Penn and I found ourselves standing alone by Casey's car. Shrieks, weeping, the
sound of feet running told us that something terrible had happened. But then, we already knew
that. Penn's face was pale and shiny with sweat.
"Maybe we should go see what's happening," he
said.

"No!" I pulled back. "Why do you always
have to do the hardest thing?" I asked fiercely.
"Why is it you who has to go to Laurie's house,

and then go over and sit with Casey's parents? Why?"

Penn looked at me helplessly. "I don't know."

A boy came running down the steps. "Don't go to the computer lab!" he cried. "Casey's killed himself."

Penn swayed, and I cried out.

"Hey, don't pass out, man," cried the boy. He grabbed Penn's arm, but Penn shook him off.

"I'm okay," he said hoarsely. "Leave me alone."

The morning passed like a dream. I went to physics class, but Dockerty didn't show up. Instead, the class stood at the windows and watched across the courtyard while white-coated men wheeled a stretcher down Haggerty's open passageway. A few moments later the door to the computer lab opened and the stretcher bumped over the door's threshold. A sheet had been spread discreetly over the body, but I could see the shape of Casey's shoes underneath, pointing up as the men pushed the stretcher down the hall.

I turned away from the window and walked out the classroom door. "Hey!" someone called after me. I went rapidly down the hall past the closed doors of the classrooms, past the stairwell and the rows of olive-colored lockers lurking in the shadows, past beds of daffodil foliage, dry as cornhusks, until I reached the administration building.

The ambulance was driving away. A clump of people had gathered on the sidewalk—Mr. Dockerty, his round glasses flashing blankly in the sunlight; the little woman from the office; Mr. Hansen, almost unrecognizable without his air of self-importance. Penn, Stephen, and Tessa stood a little apart from the others. Penn gathered me into his arms and held me tight.

The small woman from the office turned, dabbing at her eyes with a tissue. "Such a terrible tragedy," she said brokenly.

Mr. Hansen looked haunted. Even the paunch that bulged under his shirt sagged. "They had a rash of these suicides at a school in Charlotte. We're going to have to get some psychologists out here." He heaved a sigh. "Prevention, that's the ticket. I think we'd better have some workshops."

When Dockerty turned to leave, he patted Penn's shoulder awkwardly. "Don't blame yourselves," he said gruffly.

To my surprise, Tessa uttered a choked sob and then burst into tears. Stephen bent his head close to hers and murmured words of comfort.

I watched them walk away together.

I stood there a moment with Penn, neither of us saying anything. The sky was white and empty. Heat waves rose from the bare cement of the driveway, and the stark outline of the brick administration building was blurred into insignificance by my tears.

Twenty

TEEN TAKES OWN LIFE

Police were called to Barton High Monday morning when a teacher discovered the body of Casey Sean MacNamara, 17, in the school's computer lab. Police say MacNamara died of a single gunshot wound to the head. While the investigation is continuing, officials say indications are that MacNamara took his own life. A suicide note was left on the computer screen, say police. Principal Howard Hansen said MacNamara had operated the school's computer lab for the past three years. Described by Hansen as a "computer

ace," MacNamara had written many of
the programs the school uses in its day-
to-day operations. MacNamara was reported to have been despondent since
learning he was not admitted to the
Massachusetts Institute of Technology (a
prestigious college in Cambridge,
Massachusetts). Counselor Marian Healy
told the *Telegram* that Laurie Jenkins,
whose body was discovered last month at
Lookout Point, was a close friend of
MacNamara's. She believes that grief
over his friend's death may have contributed to MacNamara's depression.

Related stories, Section C, p. 5: A
CRY FOR HELP and COLLEGE ADMISSIONS
GAME—TOO STRESSFUL FOR TODAY'S
YOUTH?

The newspaper clipping was tucked in my
physics book. I treasured it as evidence that the
police considered Casey's death a suicide. The
paper already was worn from reading and reread-
ing.

After first period I looked for Stephen and
Tessa at a stairwell where they often made out.
They were standing there, hands loosely linked,

gazing into each other's eyes. They started like frightened animals when I spoke.

"Did you see the newspaper story in this morning's paper?" I asked them. "It looks like they're calling it suicide. I wonder if they're going to do an autopsy."

"I think they do in cases of suicide," Tessa said. "It's—it's routine. But maybe they've done it already. After all, the funeral is Thursday."

The MacNamaras had asked Stephen and Penn to be pallbearers. Members of the computer club were to fill out the remaining four slots.

"I wish I had a cigarette," said Stephen. "Have you talked to Penn? If we could only get out of town—to the cabin, the beach, any-where."

"Toni Andress came up to me after calculus," said Tessa. "She threw her arms around me and burst into tears. I think that's indecent, don't you? Casey didn't even know her."

Stephen's mouth twisted. "People didn't act like this when Laurie died. I don't get it."

. . . It's odd, but Casey's death seems to touch some chord that Laurie's death didn't. The entire school is in mourning. Casey was a geek while alive, but now he's some sort of

hero. Counselors are available for counsel-ing the distraught. Girls weep hysterically in the washroom, and someone has tacked a corny poem about death on the activities bulletin board.

I can't take it. . . .

Mrs. Cromarty began English class that day with a moment of silence. Then she threw the floor open for discussion of Casey's death. I sat pale and shaken at the back of the class as girls burst into tears and boys got choked up in a kind of free-floating memorial service. "I was, like, freaking out," said one girl in passionate tones, "because I'd, like, been up all night with this paper—fifteen pages—and then I couldn't get it to print." She wiped her eyes. "He figured out how to make it work. He, like, saved my life."

I felt grateful that Mr. Dockerty had chosen to stick with the scheduled class topic, though he was clearly as upset as anybody by Casey's death. The day was hard enough without listen-ing to uninhibited souls weep in class all day long.

Mysteriously, Tessa and Stephen didn't show up at the cafeteria for lunch. I was so tense that even minor variations in our usual routine frightened me.

"Why should they show up?" Penn picked at his sloppy joe with a fork. "It's not as if any of us feel like eating. I can feel people's eyes boring into me this very minute. It's like being in a cage at the zoo. I keep expecting somebody to slap a label on me—Friend of Victim, Habitat North America. I wish I could put a paper sack over my head."

"Yes, but what could Stephen and Tessa be doing?" I asked.

"Nothing worse than we've already done," he said wearily.

Nikki rested her tray on the corner of our table. "Isn't it awful?" she asked. "If only Casey'd talked to somebody. Did he ever say anything to you about wanting to kill himself?"

Penn and I shook our heads.

"I feel terrible." Nikki pressed a wadded-up napkin to her eyes. "Here I was condemning him for that stupid striptease in the cafeteria, and all the time I had no idea how he must have been suffering."

I glanced at Penn. "None of us knew, Nikki."

She squeezed my shoulder. "If you need somebody to talk to, Joanna, remember I'm here for you."

"Thank you," I said weakly.

Penn and I watched her carry her tray to a distant table filled with clones of herself, girls with cheerful smiles and carefully matched clothes.

"Stephen pointed out that everybody seems to be taking this a lot harder than they took Laurie's death," I said. "Why do you think that is?"

Penn kneaded his closed eyes. "I think it's because we've all been tempted to kill ourselves. Now that Casey's done it, for the moment it looks romantic, you know? And that's scary. Maybe kids are feeling sorry for themselves because they feel some pull to join him."

I looked at him with alarm. "You aren't thinking of that, are you, Penn?"

He smiled. "No. No, of course not."

I took hold of both his hands and held them tight.

Casey's funeral was at Lakeside Baptist Church. It seemed odd to look over from the church's parking lot and see the ducks I had fed my toast to. The front of the church had tall plate-glass windows reaching in an unbroken sweep to the point of the building. Because of the big windows, the church was full of light. I recognized many faces from school in the crowded chapel. Mr. Dockerty was sitting beside a thin, colorless woman who must be his wife. I had noticed vaguely that he wore a wedding ring, but it was difficult to imagine his having a home life and ordinary chores like taking out the garbage. I always pictured him poised like a chess piece in a pure world of physical laws, lines of force, and gravity.

The walls of the church were smooth and white. Thin narrow windows of pastel-colored glass lit the room. Behind the altar railing was a vast polished wood cross from which a sunburst of pastel rainbow colors radiated. A mound of fresh flowers rose in front of the altar railing, a startling splash of primary color amid all the white and pastel. It took a moment for me to recognize that the blanket of flowers concealed a polished wood casket. It was impossible to believe Casey was in that small casket; he had been so wild and out-of-bounds. Penn and I filed in next to Tessa and Stephen. I watched Stephen fish a small pack of nicotine gum out of his pocket. He popped one in his mouth.

"I thought you had to get a prescription for that gum," I whispered to Penn.

"I had some samples at home." He shrugged.

"But aren't you supposed to stop smoking before you use it?" I asked insistently. "What if he overdoses and has a heart attack?"

Penn glanced at him. "He won't."

The service turned out to be long. Interminable, even, as if we'd died, been sent to hell, and learned that our sentence was to listen to a never-ending sermon.

"That settles it," I told Penn as we were filing out. "I'm writing my own funeral service."

"Grotesque." Tessa shivered.

"I keep expecting Casey to pop up and say it was all a joke," said Stephen, smiling crookedly. "Weird, huh?"

I didn't think it was weird at all.

Stephen took a flask out of his pocket and quickly raised it to his lips. I saw him gulp, then stuff the flask back in his pocket. Spots of red flamed on his cheeks, but his face was pale and he was blinking rapidly.

My eyes met Penn's in alarm.

The cemetery was a plain of grass cut closely to resemble indoor-outdoor carpeting. The flat brass markers embedded in the shaved lawn were scarcely noticeable. Folding chairs had been put up under a green-striped awning, and its scalloped canvas edges fluttered in the breeze. The black hearse, black-suited attendants standing in attendance, was parked at a discreet distance. Penn, looking white as his shirt, joined the pale-faced members of the computer club who were standing beside the hearse.

"I hate this," said Tessa passionately. "It's awful, the stupid mahogany casket with the satin padding, all these flowers when nobody can possibly enjoy them." Tears streamed down her face, and I wasn't sure whether she was crying for Casey or for Stephen, who was standing with the other pallbearers, ashen and looking as if his knees might buckle any minute. "We ought to do like they do in India," she said, "and burn the stupid body."

The boys were shouldering the coffin, moving it slowly from the hearse to a stand near the canopy. I could see sweat pouring down Stephen's face and the whites of his eyes.

After the coffin was in place, I suppose the pallbearers found seats at the back of the group of chairs, because I lost sight of them. I had no difficulty recognizing Casey's mother sitting in the front row. Her pink face was swollen with tears and her eyelashes were colorless. She looked shockingly, sickeningly like Casey. Casey's little sister turned around in her seat and regarded me unblinking. With a shock I realized she was sucking on her index finger. It was as if little bits of Casey had been sown all over the cemetery and had come to life again, and I felt panic rising in my throat.

I had hated him enough to want him dead, but I was having trouble remembering that now. He seemed, in his absence, eccentric and rather lovable, a larger-than-life character who told amusing stories.

The pallbearers stepped forward again, sweating in their dark suits and ties, to lift the coffin and lower it onto the straps laid over the grave. Mrs. MacNamara plucked aimlessly at her skirt and glanced around with wild eyes. I was afraid she would try to throw herself in the grave when they lowered the coffin into it. But the moment didn't come. We signed the book and moved away, with the coffin still suspended on a web of straps over the grave. Even if someone had had the impulse to last-minute dramatics, there was no opportunity. I saw a couple of men, one of whom must have been Casey's dad, helping Mrs. MacNamara over to a black limousine.

I'm not sure what made me turn around for a

last look at the coffin. The undertaker's men were standing impassively beside the grave. A figure in black high-button shoes and a filmy long black dress stepped up to it quickly. It was Koo, her black hair lacquered and immobile in the breeze, the thin black dress fluttering behind her like a flag. She opened her hand over the coffin, and what looked like dried bits of herb pirouetted in the air and slid off the shiny coffin and disappeared. I had no idea whether her last gift to Casey was oregano and parsley or some controlled substance. The undertaker's men never blinked. I watched as she walked alone, a black figure against the plain of grass, her filmy skirt fluttering behind her.

Penn turned around and raised his eyebrows. "Coming?" he asked.

I ran to catch up.

. . . In some twisted way, Casey is more with us now than he was before he died. Before, we could get away from Casey when we liked. Now he seems to follow us everywhere. Casey haunts my troubled dreams. Sometimes I think I will never escape him.

Twenty-one

Dear Diary,
    I can't wait to go to the cabin. If the four
of us can get away for a while, I think it
may really turn us around. We've got to stop
thinking about Casey. What's past is past, I
keep telling myself. Life goes on.

The first Saturday after Casey's funeral
turned out to be a beautiful day. The sky was
robin's-egg blue. Early in the morning I had seen
the first ducklings of the season. A mother mallard waddled with five of them into the scrap of
yard that lay between our deck and the pond.
The fluffy yellow ducklings tumbled through the
grass. The doorbell rang, and I grabbed my bag
and hurried outside.

I closed my eyes as we sped away from my house. "Slow down," I said automatically. I knew Penn was speeding. He couldn't seem to help himself. The sound of the motor, the low music on the radio, began to fade out of consciousness as my body grew warm and heavy. Then, I'm not sure how, perhaps it was some quality of light through the trees, I woke up knowing that the cabin was not far ahead.

"You dozed off," said Penn. "Are you having trouble sleeping these days?" He glanced at me.

"A bit." I didn't like to go into it—the wild panic attacks when I woke up, feeling blood on my hands, the hours in the kitchen at night watching the sky grow jaundiced with the fingers of a cold dawn.

"What do you do about it?" asked Penn.

"I drink warm milk."

"I'll have to try that. I did try some sleeping-pill samples we had on hand, but"—he hesitated—"they didn't work too well."

"You can't get real sleep with sleeping pills," I said. "That REM stage is missing. That's what I read somewhere, anyway."

"No." He rubbed his temples ruefully. "Well, I can't seem to get real sleep no matter what I do."

Penn turned into the dirt drive of the cabin.

Tessa's car was parked out front, and Stephen and Tessa sat on the steps. For a fraction of a second I thought Casey was with them, and my breath sucked in sharply. "For a minute I thought—" I began, and couldn't go on.

"It's because you expect to see him," said Penn, reading my mind. "It's happened to me a hundred times." He unlocked the trunk, squinting against the sun as he glanced up at Tessa and Stephen. "I hope it wears off soon."

I was so accustomed to Tessa puttering around the kitchen that it was some time before I realized she had made no move to get up and bake bread or even mix cookie dough. She was sitting cross-legged on the floor, laying out a game of solitaire. Her short dark hair fell forward, obscuring her eyes, and I thought again how much she looked like Stephen. Both of them looked finer drawn these days. Almost gaunt. Through the big windows I could see Stephen leaning against the railing of the front stoop. He was wearing cutoffs, and one bare leg, propped on the railing, was in full sun while the other was in shade. The line of the shadow cast by the house divided him in half. A cloud of blue smoke rose over his head. Penn was sprawled in an overstuffed chair, reading a paperback with a red cover.

"Maybe I'll fix orange juice," I said. "Anybody else want some?" Penn raised his hand and smiled faintly at me.

I opened the refrigerator. The oranges were kept in the crisper. Very little else was in the refrigerator—cheese, butter, and a quart jar of cranberry juice. Casey was the only one of us who ever drank cranberry juice. I took the jar out and twisted it open. It made a soft *plopping* sound. I poured the liquid down the sink all at once. It welled up in the drain, a deep pink like watery blood, and gurgled down.

Penn came up behind me and put his arms around my waist. "What're you doing?"

I didn't answer, but I stuffed the empty jar into the trash bag.

"Oh," he said. His arms fell loosely to his side. "Did you see his book under the coffee table? Something about computers."

"Maybe we should have a yard sale," I said.

Stephen came in, bringing with him the smell of smoke. Tessa scrambled to her feet. "Maybe I'll get this junk out of the way," Stephen said. He hoisted Tessa's duffel bag over one shoulder and tucked mine under the other arm.

"No," said Penn abruptly.

They both looked at him, startled.

"Give me Joanna's," Penn said. "It goes in the big bedroom with mine."

Tessa and Stephen glanced at each other. "Well, I guess I'll bunk with Tessa, then," said Stephen.

> . . . My heart skipped a beat when Penn told Stephen that we'd be sharing a room. I'm not so much embarrassed as sad. It marks the end of a sweet dream. Once we were friends together, camping in the wilderness. Maybe that dream had never had any reality, but looking back it seems beautiful and innocent. The pretense—always in effect while Casey was alive—was that we were all equally and platonically fond of each other. . . .

That evening I lay down on the couch with my diary propped against my bent knees and tried to catch up. It seemed important to make sense of what had happened, but after a while, when I looked at the page, the letters swam before my eyes and became gibberish. I couldn't remember the code, but it didn't seem to matter.

The pen fell from my fingers and I felt myself falling. The walls of the cabin were pushed back and it became the cabin of my dreams, sweet with the smell of the aromatic chips Tessa liked to throw into the fire. I could taste strawberries and fresh bread and I felt strong and light, as if my bones were hollow and my chest muscles strong like a bird's. All I had to do was to try hard enough to lift myself up and I would be soaring over the cabin. I strained, holding my breath, and suddenly I was rising in the air. Then Casey appeared. His face was large and round, and it filled the sky like a swollen moon. His mouth was open as if he were about to speak. But something was wrong with his head!

I sat up suddenly and my diary slid to the floor. Stephen and Tessa were staring at me in alarm. Penn bent over me and stroked my hair. "It's all right," he said. "It was just a dream."

"Did I scream?" I asked.

"And how." Tessa gave a nervous titter.

"Something was wrong with his head!" I cried. I grabbed hold of Penn's arm and held on. I could feel my pulse throbbing with fear.

Stephen scrambled to his feet. "Do you have anything to drink around here, Penn?"

"Try the top shelf in the kitchen," said Penn

to my surprise. I hadn't even known liquor was kept in the cabin. I glanced over at the kitchen. Stephen gulped something clear out of a tumbler.

"Did anybody see yesterday's newspaper?" asked Tessa.

We shook our heads.

"I brought it." She disappeared into her bedroom and returned with a folded newspaper section. She handed it to Penn. "Local Girl May Be Victim of Serial Killer," read the small headline. The story went on to say that police thought there might be a link between Laurie's death and the bludgeoning death of a woman at a highway rest stop some twenty miles north of our town. This anonymous murderer, whoever he was, was leading the police away from us. I was ashamed that I felt a flash of gratitude toward him. "It looks like we're safe," said Tessa with a small sigh.

Stephen sprawled sideways in a chair. His arm was flung over the back of the chair, and his bare feet dangled in the air. He smelled richly of smoke and liquor. His face was flushed and sleepy, like a child's. "Anybody want to play Scrabble?" he asked.

Tessa produced the Scrabble box and laid out four sets of tiles.

"Seems like old times, huh?" Stephen smiled sadly. Penn shuffled off to the kitchen and brought back a bowl of potato chips. Stephen grabbed a handful clumsily, spilling several on the table. "Ho-ho," he cried. "I've got a great hand. I see a lot of possibilities here."

I glanced over at Penn. His mind wasn't on the game, and he had made no attempt to conceal his hand. I saw that he was absentmindedly arranging his tiles into a word. M-U-R-D-E-R.

A tile slipped from my fingers and fell with a clatter to the table. Penn glanced at me and quickly scrambled his tiles with his other hand.

I began to struggle to my feet. "Does anybody want anything to drink?" But Penn had his hand clasped around my forearm. I was astonished at his strength. Wordlessly he drew me down toward him. I sank to my knees next to him. He drew me close, pressing his hot hand behind my neck until our noses touched. Then he tilted my head up and kissed me full on the mouth. I could feel his tongue and taste the liquor on it. He must have felt my tremor of surprise and repulsion—I hadn't realized he had been drinking—because he let me pull away.

"Double word score," said Tessa.

"I'm getting a soda." I stood up, my eyes blurred with tears, and stumbled to the kitchen.

A minute later Penn joined me there. "Are you okay?" he asked quietly.

"I hate it when people drink," I whispered.

There was a silence.

"It's not like I've ever done it before around you," he said.

"Yes, but—"

He glanced over at Stephen and Tessa. "Let's go outside."

I grabbed my cold drink and went out the front door. Penn was barefoot, so we couldn't go far. We perched on the bottom step. The big window shed light over our heads, and we sat in a kind of artificial twilight. Mosquitoes hummed around our heads. I leaned against him, letting my tears wet his shirt. "I don't want you to be like Stephen," I choked out. "I couldn't stand it if you turned into somebody like that."

He lifted my hand and kissed it. "I'm sorry," he said. "I haven't had any sleep in so long, I don't know what I'm doing. It didn't make any sense. I don't even feel better—I feel worse."

"Penn—do you think Tessa is right?" My eyes searched his face anxiously. "Are we safe now?"

He hesitated. "I think we may be safe from the police. Is that what you mean?"

"Of course," I cried. "What else could I mean?"

"I thought you might be wondering if we're safe from Stephen."

I stared at him wide-eyed. "What are you trying to say, Penn?"

"Nothing that you don't already know," he said wearily. "He's killed two people, and we're the witnesses."

"But we're his friends!"

Penn didn't speak for a long time.

"It was an accident," I said. "They were both accidents." I remembered now that I had written in my diary that it was no accident, but the idea was so awful that I had pushed it out of my mind immediately. Suddenly my suspicions came flooding back, making me dizzy.

Penn lifted his head to look at me. He spoke so quietly, I had to strain to hear him. "Why did Stephen bring the gun with him that night, then?"

"There could be a hundred reasons," I said wildly. "He didn't mean it. He tried to keep Casey from getting the gun out of his pocket, you know that."

"Yeah, but think about it. If he had wanted

Casey to grab that jacket and get the gun, what was the best way to do it?"

Casey appeared so vividly in my mind that I gasped—Casey ferreting out secrets, zeroing in with infallible radar whenever he sensed a raw nerve. Suddenly I saw exactly what Penn was getting at. Stephen had acted alarmed and upset when Casey went for the jacket. That virtually guaranteed that nosy Casey would snatch the jacket to see what was in it.

"You see what I mean?" asked Penn quietly.

I nodded, unable to speak. I remembered the carefully indirect way Stephen and Tessa had ruined Casey's French record by "accidentally" propping it by a sunny window. Casey's murder was not so different from that, really.

"That's why I can't sleep," said Penn. "I keep replaying the whole thing in my mind and feeling like a fool. Was it really an accident that Stephen and Laurie were so close to the edge of that cliff? Or did Stephen push her over toward the cliff deliberately? They were shoving at each other, you know, and yelling, but Stephen was the stronger, heavier one. I thought he was so mad, he didn't know what he was doing, but now—"

I took a deep breath. "I'm sure it's going to be all right. I'm sure of that. You can't really think

Stephen would kill you or me, can you?"

"I don't know," he said slowly. "That's what I'm wondering. I wish I had never gotten you into this, Joanna."

I reached for him and held him, not wanting ever to let go.

When we went back into the house, I felt like a robot. I was terrified that Stephen and Tessa would notice something was wrong.

Tessa! Did she know? I remembered how she had lost her voice after Casey's murder. Had it suddenly struck her that Stephen was too "accident-prone"? Or had she been in on it from the beginning? Had they calmly hit Ping-Pong balls back and forth while they planned Casey's murder?

That night Penn and I clung to each other under the jade-green sheets. "We can't let either of them guess that we know," Penn said softly.

The curtains billowed at the open windows, moving like ghosts in the silent night breeze. My breath was shallow, and in spite of Penn's embrace my flesh felt cold. "Everything depends on it," Penn said, shivering. "That's the only way you and I are going to stay alive."

I squeezed him tight. I could feel our hearts beating in time, beating too hard. Beating with pure terror.

Don't miss ESCAPE, the next book in this thrilling series.

"Penn, my diary is missing!"

Penn's voice on the other end of the telephone line was reassuring. "Are you sure you've looked everywhere?"

"Where's to look?" I cried desperately. "I dumped out my duffel bag and it wasn't there."

The hands of the clock on the kitchen wall jerked to four o'clock.

"When did you see it last?" he asked.

"At the cabin this morning. I remember I was writing in it before breakfast. About Stephen." I gulped. "About the murders."

The silence was strained. At last, Penn said, "Are you positive you don't have it? Maybe you unpacked it and forgot."

"How could I do that?" I asked. "I only unpacked fifteen minutes ago. Look—the bag

wasn't completely zipped up. Maybe it fell out in
the trunk. Would you check?"

"Sure. I'll go out and look and get back to you."

I sat by the phone, gnawing on my knuckles,
but Penn didn't call me back, and when I dialed
his number I got no answer. I gazed forlornly out
the big window in the dining room. I should have
been worried, I suppose, about Stephen's getting
hold of my diary, but I wasn't thinking about that.
Instead, I ached at its loss. How could I get on
without it? I thought unhappily. It had been my
link to sanity in the days when I begged my father
to let me come and live with him and then struggled to make a new life for myself in yet another
strange school. I had written in my diary about the
first time Penn had kissed me and when he had
sent me red roses on Valentine's Day. I had poured
all my hopes and my nightmares onto its pages.

Minutes later, I heard Penn's car driving up. I
dashed out the front door and down the steps,
but I saw at once by his expression that he hadn't
found my diary. He climbed out of the car. "I
thought I'd come help you look," he said.

"It's not here!" I cried. "Don't you think I've
looked?"

"Then I guess we drive out to the cabin and
check there."

I climbed into Penn's car, trying to convince
myself that my diary was at the cabin. I remem-

bered stuffing it in my duffel bag before we left, but maybe I was mistaken.

As the car's engine hummed I hugged myself and my fingers kneaded the flesh of my forearm. We passed a billboard that said in large letters, "Friends don't let friends drink and drive."

Friends. The word echoed bitterly in my mind. We had been such close friends and so happy. How could it be that now we were sick with fear and eyeing each other with mistrust?

We bumped down the dirt driveway and the cabin loomed before us, its big plate-glass window flashing silver in the light.

Penn turned the key in the front door and we stepped inside. A quick glance around showed no sign of the diary, and my heart sank. Then the thorough search began. We looked under the chairs and the couch. We tossed sofa and chair cushions off and probed with our fingers in the creases of the slipcovers. In our bedroom, Penn tugged off the bed linens and checked under the pillows and bed. The other beds got the same treatment. We opened kitchen cabinets, and even looked in the refrigerator.

Penn's eyes had a look of painful concentration. "It's not here," he said at last.

"Stephen must have taken it," I said. "All he needed was a minute alone with my duffel bag while we were carrying things to the car. He's seen me stuff my diary in on top of my clothes lots of times. He'd know right where to look for it. I feel so stupid! Leaving my bag unwatched like that! Dumb!" I slapped my forehead.

Penn stood up. "There's nothing we can do about it now," he said. "Let's go back to town and get something to eat."

We were both silent on the drive back to town. Penn actually slowed down to thirty-five when the speed limit changed at the city limits, which showed how shaken he was. "Welcome to Barton City," said the sign. It was covered with tarnished medallions the size of plates. Kiwanis Club, Elks Club, Rotary Club welcomed us. A spray of wild roses spilled over the signs, its pink matching the faded rose of a crushed fried chicken carton that lay on the grass.

"Maybe for now," Penn suggested hesitantly, "you could drive to school a different way. Maybe you should change the route you take when you go to classes, too. You know?"

"Next, we get matching bulletproof vests," I said.

"Seriously, we don't know what he might try next," said Penn.

"Maybe we're panicking for no reason."

"Maybe. But we can't count on it. Remember how he kept harping on whether Casey was going to turn state's evidence? He's got to be thinking the same thing about us."

Especially if he reads my diary, I thought miserably.

"I remember he sat up all night trying to think of some exotic poison that would kill Casey without leaving a trace," said Penn bitterly. "For all I know he's getting ready to sprinkle arsenic on our meat loaf."

"He's not going to do that. He'll think up something new, not something he talked to you about."

"I'm not sure of anything. What I keep thinking is that it must be a lot easier to kill when you're doing it for the third time."

This gloomy observation put a damper on any further conversation. It seemed crazy to be going on with our lives as if nothing had happened when we might be being pursued by a murderer.

"So what exactly is in this diary of yours?" Penn asked after a while.

"Everything!"

"You mean you've put in everything we've been talking about—about Laurie's and Casey's murders?" He glanced at me quickly.

I nodded.

"I thought you were always behind when it came to writing in your diary. How come all of a sudden you're caught up?"

I licked my lips. "Writing in it calms me down. When I woke up early yesterday, I sat up in the bed and wrote for quite a while. But it was in code, Penn. That's why I wasn't worried about it. Every word I've written in it has been in code."

"I hope it's a good code," he said.

At school the next morning, I came upon Stephen and Tessa making out in the shadows of a stairwell. I wasn't sure whether I should speak to them or not. But before I could decide, Stephen turned around to face me. "Hold up, Joanna." His tone was offhand. "I've got something for you." He rummaged in his book bag, then made a pitching gesture. My diary spun in the air and landed in my outstretched hands.

"I don't know how it ended up in my bag," he said. "I guess I was packing in too much of a hurry yesterday."

"Thanks," I whispered.

Without looking back, I fled.